The Boarding-

》》》》》》》》》》 《《《《《《《《《《《

Nadezhda Khvoshchinskaya

The
Boarding-
School Girl

TRANSLATED FROM THE RUSSIAN, ANNOTATED, AND
WITH AN INTRODUCTION BY KAREN ROSNECK

NORTHWESTERN UNIVERSITY PRESS
EVANSTON, ILLINOIS

》》》》》》》》》》 《《《《《《《《《《《

Northwestern University Press
www.nupress.northwestern.edu

First published in Russian in 1861 under the title "Pansionerka," in *Otechestvennye zapiski*. Published in *Povesti i rasskazy* in 1984 by Moskovskii rabochii. English translation copyright © 2000 by Northwestern University Press. Published 2000. All rights reserved.

Printed in the United States of America

10 9 8 7 6 5 4 3 2

ISBN-13: 978-0-8101-1744-0
ISBN-10: 0-8101-1744-4

Library of Congress Cataloging-in-Publication Data

Krestovskii, V., 1824–1889.
    [Pansionerka. English]
    The boarding-school girl / Nadezhda Khvoshchinskaya ; translated from the Russian, annotated, and with an introduction by Karen Rosneck.
    p. cm.
    ISBN 0-8101-1744-4 (paper)
    I. Rosneck, Karen. II. Title.
PG3337.K42 P3613 1999
891.73'3—dc21   99-050310
                                                          CIP

»»» CONTENTS «««

»»» ACKNOWLEDGMENTS «««

I want to take this opportunity to express my thanks to the many people who generously assisted in making this book. I'm greatly indebted to Michael Katz for his direction, advice, and corrections in preparing both the introduction and translation. Much of the cohesiveness of the text as a whole can be attributed to the influence of his experience and skill as a translator, a critic, and an editor.

I am also very grateful to Mary Zirin for her corrections and innumerable excellent suggestions for improving the final draft of both the translation and the introduction. Thanks to Jehanne Gheith for her insightful comments and criticisms of drafts of the introduction, and to my English editor, Lisa Chipongian, for identifying and reworking infelicitous language usage in both the translation and the introduction. I am also grateful to Valentina Pogosyan for combing through the translation with a native speaker's command of Russian to help fine-tune word choice and identify errors. Our many hours of discussion resulted in countless refinements to the translation as well as many fine memories. My thanks to Elena Melikian, Saule Omarova, and Alexander Greshaev for providing occasional translation advice and suggestions as well, and to the staff of the Interlibrary Loans Department of Memorial Library for obtaining the rare volume not already available among the research collections at the University of Wisconsin. Finally, I want to extend my thanks to my friends but also my parents, Paul H. and Violet B. Rosneck, for their interest, encouragement, and support throughout the duration of my work on this project.

Karen Rosneck

> The reader expects very simple, universal and con-
> ventional goals [from a literary work]: the truthful re-
> production of reality and the stimulation of serious
> thought in society about that reality. To determine if
> these goals will be accomplished, the reader tries to
> select literary works least subject to objections and
> contradictions, written, so to speak, by specialists, ex-
> perts in the field, for example, novels about women,
> written by women.
>> —V. Krestovsky-pseudonym [Nadezhda
>> Khvoshchinskaya]

Literary history preserves the memory of many of the finest feminine portraits created by nineteenth-century Russian authors. The
work of well-known writers such as Pushkin, Turgenev, Dostoevsky, and Tolstoy still charm readers with their powerfully and vi-
brantly rendered fictional heroines. A diverse, celebrated assort-
ment of feminine virtues and vices, these Tatyanas, Elenas, Sonyas,
and Annas share one common characteristic: none were created by
women writers. Confronted with this fact, the contemporary reader must conclude that the gift of depicting nineteenth-century
Russian women's reality had been bestowed only upon men or that
there simply had been no women writers in Russia to undertake
this task.

Fortunately, neither conclusion has proved true. The achieve-
ments of women writers in the latter half of the eighteenth century

paved the way for a tremendous growth in women's writing in the nineteenth. Women like Anna Bunina, Nadezhda Teplova, Evdokiya Rostopchina, and Karolina Pavlova built a strong foundation for women's writing in Russia largely as poets in the first third of the nineteenth century. The growing preference for prose among readers and writers beginning in the 1830s attracted the contributions of a new constellation of authors, including Elena Gan, Marya Zhukova, and Nadezhda Durova. All of these women fought successfully to gain entrance onto the Russian literary arena, developing themes and images that became central to succeeding generations of women writers in Russia.[1]

Nadezhda Dmitrievna Khvoshchinskaya was one of the most successful women writers of the nineteenth century. During the course of a career that spanned over forty years, from 1842 to 1889, her wide-ranging literary work included poetry, prose, drama, children's literature, translations, and critical articles. An heir of this first generation of Russian women poets and prose writers, Khvoshchinskaya earned the respect and admiration of readers and critics over the course of a long literary career. Enjoying considerable popularity as a writer during her lifetime, she nonetheless shared the fate of her female predecessors. Her memory vanished from literary history at the close of the century.[2]

The absence of Khvoshchinskaya's name among the pages of Russian literary history represents a particular misfortune for present-day readers, literary historians, and critics alike. Her humorous and spirited prose style, lively imagination, and radical approach to contemporary themes and intellectual trends offer rich rewards. Her sharp analytical skills and close attention to psychological detail provide a fascinating glimpse of Russian life in the nineteenth century. Khvoshchinskaya's short novel *The Boarding-School Girl* (*Pansionerka*) represents one of the best examples of her innovative talent.

Khvoshchinskaya was born May 20, 1824, in the Russian province of Ryazan. The modest gentry family environment must have been conducive to the development of literary talent: two of Khvoshchinskaya's younger sisters, Sofya and Praskovya, also became writers.[3] Nadezhda and Sofya established a close relationship in early childhood; as adults, the two sisters formed a productive literary partnership, sharing ideas for present and future work. Because of her poor health and her family's insufficient means, Khvoshchinskaya received most of her formal education at home from private tutors; she attended a private boarding school only briefly, between the ages of eleven and twelve.

While she later established her literary reputation as a prose writer, Khvoshchinskaya began her career as a poet. Her first published poem appeared in the journal *Son of the Fatherland* (*Syn otechestva*) in 1842 when she was eighteen years old. *The Literary Gazette* (*Literaturnaya gazeta*) published additional poetry in 1847. Although she wrote over a hundred poems during her lifetime, most have never been published. Her lifelong desire to publish her poems together in a separate edition has never been realized.

Khvoshchinskaya's first prose work, the short novel *Anna Mikhailovna*, appeared in *Notes of the Fatherland* (*Otechestvennye zapiski*) in 1850. She adopted the masculine pseudonym V. Krestovsky to publish this novella, subsequently retaining its use for all of her prose fiction. Refusing to relinquish her pseudonym even when the work of another writer with the same name (Vsevolod Krestovsky) appeared in print, she simply appended the qualifier "pseudonym" to her pen name to reduce future confusion. Later in her career she adopted additional masculine pseudonyms to publish her critical essays.[4]

Khvoshchinskaya apparently enjoyed a happy childhood and youth despite the family's prolonged periods of financial hardships. When she was still a child, her father lost his civil service position after he was accused of embezzlement; subsequent legal proceedings deprived him of a large sum of money, forcing him to sell his property. He vigorously maintained his innocence over a period of fifteen years while struggling to regain financial security. Although he obtained another stable position in 1845, the family's financial recovery was fleeting. He died in 1856, leaving the struggling gentry family in yet another precarious economic situation. In the following years Khvoshchinskaya assumed a leading role in family decisions and economic support and, up until the 1880s, lived almost exclusively in Ryazan. She wrote the greatest portion of her literary work in a separate room, at the little desk that her father had given her. She and Sofya left Ryazan infrequently, usually visiting literary and artistic friends and acquaintances in the cultural center of Petersburg only once a year. Among her Petersburg friends numbered Ivan Turgenev and the poet Nikolay Shcherbina.[5]

Appearing in 1861 in the progressive journal *Notes of the Fatherland, The Boarding-School Girl* claimed immediate popularity with readers. Khvoshchinskaya's vibrant and memorable depiction of the educational experiences of her fifteen-year-old heroine, Lolenka, especially resonated with contemporary girls and women. Her portrayal of her young heroine's independent working life in Petersburg in 1860 presented an early fictional example of emerging new roles for women in Russian society.

While many readers responded enthusiastically to *The Boarding-School Girl,* some apparently found aspects of the novella confusing and even disappointing. Stepan Dudyshkin, editor and critic for *Notes of the Fatherland,* wrote to Khvoshchinskaya on March 2, 1861, soon after the appearance of the novella. Acquainting her with some readers' interpretations of the novella, Dudyshkin expresses confidence in his knowledge of the author's intentions. His letter ambiguously chides the public's obtuseness and gently criticizes the ending as perhaps too unclear. He suggests that

Khvoshchinskaya might obtain even greater success in the future by complying with the public's taste for greater clarity and positive images of contemporary working women.

Everyone is praising *The Boarding-School Girl*, and everyone is dissatisfied with the ending. This has angered me, and in arguments I began to recognize that the ending of the novella is being understood in another way completely—that is, as if you had wanted to depict an ideal contemporary working woman. As funny as this may seem, nevertheless, I felt obliged to reread the ending and found that, really, it could be much more developed. And if you take advantage of it, you'll have brilliant success. The opinion of the public is always worth something, even if they don't understand the work.[6]

Khvoshchinskaya examined her reasons for writing *The Boarding-School Girl* in a letter to a female friend in 1865. Her remarks seem to confirm Dudyshkin's assertion that the depiction of an ideal working woman was not one of her objectives. While expressing disapproval for some of her heroine's decisions in the novella, Khvoshchinskaya's comments suggest a broader plan for her work: the exploration of various means to advance social progress.

It's possible, as I said in *The Boarding-School Girl*, to leave one's stupid, cruel parents, reject attachments, go to work, but this will only be half a life, even an abnormal one, and contains its own sorrows and discomforts. In my opinion, any rupture causes sorrow, discomfort, disorder, but never the orderly structuring of life or society.[7]

Although Khvoshchinskaya's work continued to garner approval from the reading public, and especially women, reviews remained infrequent and rarely enthusiastic.[8] Many critics found her plots and themes, focusing on provincial women's lives and family conflicts, monotonous and limited in scope.[9] Writer Evgeniya Tur expressed her impatience with the lack of critical attention to Khvoshchinskaya's prose fiction in an essay written in 1861. She complained that Khvoshchinskaya's "remarkable works have somehow gone unnoticed, unmentioned. The collection of short novels in four volumes that appeared last year went unmentioned. Meanwhile the public reads them with pleasure. . . ."[10] In an article for *The Contemporary* (*Sovremennik*) in 1864 Mikhail Saltykov (Shchedrin) described Khvoshchinskaya as a "very gifted" writer but criticized her prose for its excessive attention to psychological detail (a deficiency he also attributed to the work of Charlotte Brontë and George Eliot in the same article). He argued that her emphasis on psychological analysis has deprived her of "the success that belongs to her by right of her talent."[11]

The immense popularity of Khvoshchinskaya's novel *Ursa Major* (*Bol'shaya medveditsa*) (1871) and critical acclaim over the series of stories published under the title *Album. Groups. Portraits* (*Albom. Gruppy. Portrety*) (1874–78) boosted her career to some prominence in the 1870s and 1880s.[12] Critic Mikhail Protopopov compared Krestovsky's talent with that of her literary contemporaries in an article written for *Russian Wealth* (*Russkoe bogatstvo*) in 1880:

The talent of V. Krestovsky is the kind that, in Russia, in particular, is a rare gift that doesn't weaken but strengthens over time. . . . In the essence of his talent, Krestovsky isn't one of those writers who produces a fanfare in literature. His work says a lot to the attentive reader, but doesn't strike the attention of the unattentive reader. Figuratively speaking, he doesn't use bright colors in his palette like Count Tolstoy or even Pisemsky. He doesn't polish his work like Turgenev or Goncharov. There is none of the eccentricity in his manner or originality of plot characteristic of Dostoevsky. He stands out from our "pleiades," as Ostrovsky and Shchedrin stand out from him. V. Krestovsky never, so to speak, shouts or gesticulates. He speaks with an even, although soft, but always firm and sure voice. There are no excesses of passion, but unwavering and stubborn feeling, hope in love. . . .[13]

Other favorable reviews followed. In 1880 writer Petr Boborykin declared in the journal *Cause* (*Delo*) that "such a woman writer as Krestovsky has no equal now in Western Europe, with the exception of George Eliot."[14]

At this time Khvoshchinskaya also received a number of special honors recognizing her lasting success as a writer. In 1883 the literary world organized a formal tribute to her career. Author and playwright Nadezhda Merder presented a welcoming opening statement to a gathering of mostly women; author and critic Marya Tsebrikova offered an appraisal of Khvoshchinskaya's work:

Dear Nadezhda Dmitrievna! . . . Today, admirers of your talent and representatives of several generations greet you. Such unanimity is possible only when an artist has touched a deep common chord, when his work, reflecting the wrongs of the day, propels us toward a better future. You expressed hope for this better future as well as a longing for it and charted the inclinations which promise it. Many aspects of our social life have been reflected in your work; with keen and implacable analysis you have exposed every lie and the self-interested phrase-mongering that disguises service to an idea. You are one of the first to offer your voice to advocate for a woman's right to participate in the public sphere; with deep understanding of a woman's heart you presented many true and artistic depictions of her battle and suffering. If this battle may be considered won to a certain degree, it's only because there have been women like you who knew how to show that the common cause was their cause.[15]

Tsebrikova's remarks offer a glimpse at the reception of Khvoshchinskaya's work among contemporary readers. Praising her honesty, analytical skill, and mastery in depicting women's lives through her fiction, Tsebrikova particularly emphasized Khvoshchinskaya's impact as a role model and proponent for women's rights. Her comments demonstrate the powerful resonance that the example of Khvoshchinskaya's life and work evoked among female readers.

After her mother's death in May 1884, Khvoshchinskaya left Ryazan altogether, moving to Petersburg in the fall. Living modestly, she maintained a strict routine, getting up early and immediately sitting down to work. The habit of saving paper, acquired during her frugal childhood, also encouraged the development of her characteristic diminutive handwriting. At the end of her work day she busied herself with needlework, a lifelong pastime.

Khvoshchinskaya's health steadily deteriorated during her sixties. The deforming curvature of her spine, an outcome of rickets in childhood, exacerbated heart and pulmonary conditions, including emphysema. Struggling over the course of her career to support herself with her writing, she never completely escaped poverty. She died in a summer cottage in Petergof (now Staryi Petergof) outside Petersburg on June 8, 1889.

Russian Politics and Women's Education

In writing about women's education in *The Boarding-School Girl*, Khvoshchinskaya treated one of the most central issues of what became known as the "woman question" in Russia. While promising the pleasures of fictional entertainment, her novella also succinctly presented the substance of current debate about women's education, linking abstract philosophical ideas to concrete Russian sociopolitical events. Set in 1852 and 1860, the novella touched upon a variety of influences that guided the course of contemporary discussion, including trends in the government's educational philosophy, the superficiality of traditional school curriculum, and the educational impact of women's employment as nurses during the Crimean War.

The structural and philosophical basis for girls' secondary education in Russia originated in the eighteenth century. State-operated boarding schools, or institutes, designed in conformity with French models, were established by Catherine the Great in 1764 for daughters of the nobility to help cultivate better citizens and mothers. As a means to mold behavior and maintain discipline, the institutes advocated complete separation of the students from their families throughout the entire seven to nine years or more course of study.[16] The institutes became firmly established in Russia in the eighteenth century and continued to prosper in the nineteenth, despite growing criticism of the superficiality of the schools' curriculum and the restrictive conditions of institute life. Completely isolated from the world outside the school's walls and immersed in a narrow field of instruction that stressed moral rectitude and good behavior, the girls attending these schools graduated with little practical life experience. The restrictive conditions within the institutes prevailed well into the nineteenth century: weekend, summer, and holiday vacations were sanctioned only in 1864. The state finally established full day schools for girls at the secondary level only in 1858.[17]

Arising in the eighteenth century at much the same time as the institutes, private boarding schools offered another option for well-to-do families seeking educational opportunities for their daughters. These schools especially flourished in the early nineteenth century by pursuing aggressive strategies to insure their survival. In order to increase student enrollment among poorer gentry families, private boarding schools charged reduced fees for students attending school as semiboarding, or day, students. While usually offering a similarly superficial curriculum, these schools often adopted less restrictive measures than the institutes, yielding to family pressure for greater contact between the students and their families throughout the school year.

Taking place during the reigns of Nicholas I and Alexander II, the events in *The Boarding-School Girl* occur in a period of sweeping changes in national politics and increased public attention to women's education. Nicholas came to power on the eve of the Decembrist Uprising in 1825, establishing a government that maintained especially strict controls over most aspects of Russian life. The 1848 overthrow of King Louis Philippe in France, which sparked revolutionary movements throughout Europe, only increased the czar's fears of social upheaval in Russia. In response, Nicholas initiated a concentrated program of political repression. The numerous political circles that had formed in the more relaxed political climate of the 1840s became a particular focus of government oppression. Members of subversive political groups were exiled to the Caucasus or Siberia;[18] by 1850 at least twelve agencies formed a system of strict censorship. Searching for "double meanings," censors scoured literary works, a traditional mode of political expression in czarist Russia.

The death of Nicholas I in 1855 and Russian defeat in the Crimean War the following year introduced much needed catalysts for change. While the military defeat did not threaten the country's security, the war did effectively destroy national confidence. The more progressive political climate established during the reign of Alexander II encouraged a reevaluation of Russian social and political life to help explain Russia's failure and promote new directions for change.

The spectrum of issues that emerged as the "woman question" in Russia flowered into public debate after 1855. Accounts of the participation of women as nurses with the Sisters of Mercy during the Crimean War sparked a broad examination of women's roles in

Russian life. The nurses' wartime service demonstrated the potential value of women's contributions to society through work outside the home. Discussion about work in turn triggered intense debate about means to improve women's educational preparation for assuming new roles beyond the domestic sphere.[19]

The events depicted in *The Boarding-School Girl* suggest a complex interrelationship between national politics and women's changing roles during this period. Lolenka's evolving relationship in 1852 with her neighbor, Veretitsyn, a political exile, powerfully affects the direction of her formal educational experiences. Criticizing her very circumscribed world of school and family, Veretitsyn unknowingly exerts a powerful influence on his young pupil's decision to adopt an independent working life in Petersburg eight years later.

Khvoshchinskaya's novella specifically addresses issues central to contemporary debate about women's education. Problems of public concern, including the superficiality of traditional school curriculum and the practice of isolating students from their families within closed boarding schools such as the institutes, play a significant role in the novella. The heroine, fifteen-year-old Lolenka, a day student at a private boarding school, receives her formal education at school while still living at home with her family. The shifting narrative perspective between home and school encourages the comparison of lessons offered by both environments. Khvoshchinskaya's examination of her protagonists' lives eight years after the novella opens, in 1860, reveals dramatic changes in Russian life and women's roles.

The Boarding-School Girl

First published in 1861, *The Boarding-School Girl* immediately joined a rather large family of well-known and much honored Russian literary works devoted to the theme of women and education.

Khvoshchinskaya's novella reveals a substantial debt to illustrious, largely male, literary predecessors from Pushkin to Goncharov while presenting a fresh reworking of this theme. Tracing the influence of books and reading on the young and impressionable feminine mind, Khvoshchinskaya transforms familiar material while introducing significant innovations in both the form and content of her novella.

The subject of women's education remained a persistent fascination for Russian writers throughout the nineteenth century. Not simply an isolated literary preoccupation, the subject also generated intense interest among the general public. The slow but steady increase in the number of schools for girls, as well as the number of students attending these schools during the early nineteenth century, resulted in debate over the advantages and hazards of formal education for women.

Khvoshchinskaya addressed the theme of women's education in Russian literature in an essay written in 1862, noting the ubiquitous and central role of a male mentor as a guide for a young woman's education:

> But the education of young women exclusively by means of reading Russian novels (when her whole preparation for this consists of a single Russian grammar, her education must be limited)—this is an invention of literary authors. These authors make use of this every time they suddenly need a female citizen-butterfly to appear from the rural chrysalid. And it always turns out badly. In aiding this transformation there is always a guide, always of the male sex. . . .[20]

The central role of a male mentor in guiding a young woman's reading proclivities undeniably recurs with astonishing regularity in Russian novels of the nineteenth century. The ubiquitous presence of male mentor figures in Russian literature during this period suggests the preoccupation of literary authors with the social changes altering women's roles in Russian life. Indeed, the "woman question" also directly affected male authors. Increased female literacy helped promote the appearance of significant numbers of women writers for the first time in Russian history. The relationship between the male mentor and his young, untutored female pupil explores the changing literary face of masculine privilege to education as well as to authorship.

Examples of this typology abound in Russian literature. Through her father's indifference and careless lack of vigilance, Pushkin's Tatyana in *Eugene Onegin* (1825–32) indiscriminately peruses both Richardson and Rousseau. Later in the novel, the now bookish Tatyana attempts to understand Onegin's behavior, which by then includes murder, through a thorough and secret examination of his personal library.[21] Tatyana obtains her reading pleasure clandestinely in the absence of appropriate supervision and guidance. Her transformation from an artless, naive, impulsive girl to a studied, sophisticated young socialite is facilitated by her introduction to artifice through reading.[22]

Tatyana's sister, Olga, is more fortunate in her access to instructional guidance. Her discriminating suitor, Lensky, prudently selects conventionally appropriate moralistic novels to read aloud, carefully and judiciously omitting passages "unfit for maiden's heart or head."[23] His discriminating knowledge of literature and heedful diligence in molding wholesome attitudes in the mind of the weaker sex preserve Olga from the unsound and even lawless influences to which her sister falls prey. Still, Olga benefits little from the devoted efforts of a male mentor. A shallow, self-absorbed, superficial young lady, her character evinces little emotional development; throughout the novel, her model of behavior remains considerably less attractive than that of her sister.[24]

In his novel *Polinka Saks* (1847), Alexander Druzhinin produced a heroine who realized too late her good luck in possessing an unusually deserving and enthusiastic mentor for a husband. For all of Saks's eagerness to inculcate the value of book learning to his wife, Polinka remains stubbornly self-willed, impervious, and uninterested in his efforts. With Saks's blessings she abandons her husband for a less altruistic and less pedagogical dandy, only to recognize her mistake later.

Goncharov's Olga in *Oblomov* (1859) receives insufficient reading supervision from a largely indifferent aunt. Falling in love with Oblomov, Olga nearly overwhelms him with her enthusiasm for reading and learning, begging him to lend her books and discuss their content. She later abandons hope of marriage to the irresolute Oblomov and finds happiness married to his more decisive and energetic friend Stolz. After years of marriage, Stolz maintains an active influence on his wife as a mentor and is still able to "throw some new, bold idea, some acute observation on life into her eager and receptive mind. . . ."[25]

The Boarding-School Girl represents a significant departure from its predecessors in the debate over women's education.[26] Khvoshchinskaya's fresh reworking of the male mentor's role in guiding her young heroine's educational progress contrasts sharply with the work of her predecessors. Veretitsyn, the male mentor in Khvoshchinskaya's novella, doesn't merely dispense reading matter appropriate for developing delicate feminine sensibilities like Lensky, Oblomov, and Saks. His radical approaches toward learning and literary representation provoke his young pupil's rebellion against unjust authority at home as well as at school. Khvoshchinskaya's examination of the literary representation of knowledge and "truth" through the character of Veretitsyn forms the basis for her innovative use of language in the novella as well.

At first glance, Veretitsyn seems an unlikely candidate for a mentor. A poor authority as a teacher, he reveals his imperfect knowledge of German, incorrectly reciting the title of a waltz by Lanner.[27]

Even worse, he reveals his poor knowledge of Russian literature, confusing poetry by the eighteenth-century Russian poets Dimitriev and Kheraskov.[28] Fortunately, Veretitsyn's strength as a mentor does not rely upon his limited storehouse of knowledge. Sent to the city of N. for crimes associated with his poetry, Veretitsyn poses a subversive threat to society and a challenge to established authority. Not surprisingly, Veretitsyn advocates unorthodox educational methodologies as well. In challenging Lolenka to evaluate what she's learned at school, not simply memorize, Veretitsyn reveals his skepticism of the "truths" presented in books, while emphasizing the value of subjective interpretation as an intrinsic part of learning.

Veretitsyn particularly criticizes Lolenka's mindless memorization of the names and deeds of "great men" that forms the basis of her boarding-school education. In questioning textbook representations of knowledge, he challenges her to think critically, musing, "You'll understand, God forbid, that one great man was a petty tyrant, another a scoundrel, a third sinless only because he had no opportunity to sin." For Veretitsyn, Lolenka's textbooks claim an objective representation of reality that masks their function as instruments of indoctrination. The powerful enjoy the privilege of authorship as a means to control public opinion, obscure wrongdoing, mask personal failings, and depict social inequities as immutable truths in order to justify their own positions of power.

A social and political outsider, Veretitsyn nonetheless still enjoys the freedoms and privileges offered to men in Russian society. In exposing the illusory nature of the "truths" presented in Lolenka's textbooks as a form of social conditioning, Veretitsyn also implicitly criticizes the "truths" that sustain masculine privilege while justifying women's continued relegation to traditional roles within the family. Veretitsyn's relationships with Lolenka, his young neighbor, and Sofya, the woman he loves, constitute a practical testing ground for his theoretical convictions about human freedom and equality. Meeting by chance after a separation of eight years, Lolenka and Veretitsyn renew their past discussions about women, work, social change, and social commitment. Veretitsyn's apparent disapproval of Lolenka's independent working life in Petersburg leads her to contemplate with dismay the possibility that her former mentor has abandoned his radical views.

The introduction of female mentor figures in *The Boarding-School Girl* represents a significant innovation in the literary debate over women and education. The influence of feminine mentors in the novella refutes predecessors' depictions of the heroine as an "empty slate" awaiting the Pygmalion-like transforming influence of a male mentor. Khvoshchinskaya unmasks the arrogance of the male mentor who presumes sole responsibility for forming the mind of a young untutored girl.

The contributions of female mentor figures occupy a central role in shaping the views and perspectives of Khvoshchinskaya's heroine. Lolenka's unrelenting disdain for Sofya Khmelevskaya's model of behavior in the last chapter of the novella only confirms Sofya's powerful influence on the young heroine. Lolenka's remarks to Veretitsyn reveal how much her image of both herself and Sofya as victims of their love for Veretitsyn has since restructured her life. She concludes that all relationships are a painful "yoke" that should be cast off in search of greater personal freedom. Veretitsyn, still in love with Sofya, continues to argue as he had earlier in the novella, that Sofya's capacity for self-sacrifice and devotion to others conclusively demonstrates her superiority over other women.

At the same time, the opinions expressed by Veretitsyn's friend, Ibrayev, seem to confirm Lolenka's dim view of Sofya's value as a role model. An ambitious, newly established member of N.'s bureaucratic elite, Ibrayev arrogantly presumes Sofya's pleasure at the possibility of his visits to her home since she "wouldn't be opposed, of course, to an advantageous match." Her marriage to a local landowner seems at once to confirm Ibrayev's suspicions of her calculating designs to snare a husband, Veretitsyn's belief in her self-sacrificing "perfection," and Lolenka's conviction that Sofya simply fears greater personal independence and freedom. An object of analysis throughout the novella, Sofya eludes the simplistic judgments of both readers and other characters. Most of the events in her life as well as her own justification for her behavior remain beyond the boundaries of the text.

Another powerful feminine influence on the young heroine throughout the novella, Lolenka's mother claims a dominant role in molding her daughter's views and perspectives. The embroidery work that she assigns to Lolenka, while an expression of women's relegation to traditional roles within the family, also represents a heritage of cultural creativity transmitted from mother to daughter over generations. An "expert" in the domestic arts, Lolenka's mother guides her daughter's creative sensibility until Lolenka's growing rebellion against superficiality and injustice at school and at home begins to reveal itself in an embroidery design that has gone awry, crooked. However, Lolenka's mother also reveals her complicity in sustaining women's oppression: she conceals from Lolenka the fact that she has been set to work sewing her own dowry.[29]

Throughout the course of the novella, Lolenka diligently works at her embroidery frame, fashioning a design for a dickey that she intends to give to her mother. Although she spends much of her time throughout the novella working at her embroidery frame, the design that Lolenka weaves ultimately remains concealed from the reader. Her embroidery design also figuratively suggests the outlines of Khvoshchinskaya's own novelistic construction. Similarly, the author superficially reveals her novelistic stitchery through plot and character, while only suggesting her thematic intentions.[30]

Khvoshchinskaya's exploration of the literary representation of knowledge and truth in *The Boarding-School Girl* establishes a theoretical basis for her innovative use of language in the novella as well. She fashions her own creative response to Veretitsyn's criticism of Lolenka's textbooks by creating a text that self-consciously resists the false appearance of authority and objectivity. Employing irony to undermine the authority of her third-person narrator, confusing meaning in dialogue, and positioning fragments and ellipsis points to leave statements and thoughts open-ended, Khvoshchinskaya constructs a text that resists easy interpretation.

Khvoshchinskaya skillfully wields language to undermine the appearance of an unbiased, omniscient narrative voice. The ironic treatment of characters and events subverts the impression of a single, objective narrative frame of reference. Narrative discourse uncomfortably disintegrates into nonsense while subjective commentary and judgment repeatedly interrupt psychological analysis. The narrator digresses at the beginning of the second chapter of the novella with an analysis of the nature of courage, citing the experience of soldiers in battle as an example, only to invalidate the entire digression nonsensically by suddenly stating, "Courage doesn't exist." In the very next paragraph a digressive, apparently objective, abstract examination of boredom and inactivity suddenly nullifies its appearance of impartiality with the interjection of subjective judgment: "All of this is bad, but condemning it would be cruel." The narrator's taste for contradiction and logical absurdity continually erodes the appearance of an objective, neutral representation of reality.

Khvoshchinskaya also undermines readers' expectations of a single authoritative narrative frame of reference by mixing the voice of her third-person narrator with the judgments and opinions of other characters.[31] Lolenka's mother fusses over her daughter's attire at the beginning of chapter 8 as the family prepares to attend a church service. The third-person omniscient narrator lists the clothing accessories that Lolenka's mother selects for her daughter, including a little tie "that would probably look nice on Lolenka because Lolenka was a brunette." This subjective judgment, trailing at the end of a sequence of third-person omniscient narration, logically belongs to Lolenka's mother. Thinking aloud or to herself as she sorts through clothing, Lolenka's mother justifies her decision to select the tie. The blending of third-person omniscient narration with the voice of Lolenka's mother, without any marker indicating the presence of reported speech, generates an ambiguity in perspective that undermines readers' expectations of a single, authoritative narrative viewpoint.

Khvoshchinskaya's characters, like her narrator, stubbornly resist rigid definitions and fixed identity. The frequent use of ellipsis in dialogues allows characters' thoughts and utterances to trail off beyond the boundaries of the text. Dialogues sometimes generate ambiguities that lead both reader and characters into confusion and misunderstanding. When Lolenka asks Veretitsyn if the play by Shakespeare that he has offered to lend her can be read (*mozhno chitat'*), he mistakenly assumes she is asking whether the play will be difficult or even interesting to read. The intended meaning of her question, whether the play represents the kind of wholesome reading permissible for her to read, becomes clear only when she corrects him.

Khvoshchinskaya's novella about girls and education mimics and parodies contemporary educational methodology and practice. Repetition within sentences or paragraphs recalls Lolenka's textbook recitations as she prepares for her exams. Characters affect pedagogical posturing, frequently delivering lectures to one another. The boarding school's hierarchical grading system resonates throughout the novella in spatial references to "high" and "low," in a preoccupation with getting ahead, in promotions. Khvoshchinskaya ascribes a major role to cultural conditioning for molding and preserving public acceptance of social hierarchy and sexual inequity.

The Boarding-School Girl represents a radical departure from previous depictions of the relationship between women and education in Russian literature. Adopting the familiar presence of a male mentor as a guide for her young heroine's formal education, Khvoshchinskaya creates a spokesman for radical approaches to learning and literary representation. Indeed, Veretitsyn's educational influence incites Lolenka to question her textbooks' apparent objectivity and claims to authority. Female mentor figures play an important role in the novella as well, presenting complex, contrasting role models and introducing the possibility of distinct feminine cultural traditions of creativity. Rejecting the representation of absolute values of truth while stressing the validity of subjective interpretation, Khvoshchinskaya challenges the reader to question the text and characters as well as the nature of truth itself.

Writing to a female friend in 1865, Khvoshchinskaya specifically considers her intentions in exploring women's lives in her fiction.

> You say that in my novels I have indicated a new path for women. No, my friend, you are mistaken. A new existence, perhaps. Woman will never discover a path forward alone, by herself; the whole general structure of life must help her. . . . I have simply described the position of woman as it has been, as it often is now. The anguish of this position is only a consequence of the whole environment. I have shown a sacrifice so the guilty will see where they've brought things, and, having thought about it, will perhaps start to live more sensibly. Look at my literary work from this point of view and you'll

become convinced that I am not a "bold guide to new paths," but an unsuccessful pedagogue to whom no one listened and no one will listen. I can't show any path because, under the present conditions of society, I don't see any myself, and, not believing in what is called "progress, steps forward," I don't even dare say if this path exists.[32]

Khvoshchinskaya's description of herself as a writer "to whom no one listened and no one will listen" contrasts incongruously with the reality of her own literary popularity and success. Rather than self-deprecating modesty, the incongruity of her statement may instead suggest subtle wit. A woman writer, Khvoshchinskaya remained an outsider, "no one" in relation to the dominant masculine literary establishment. The masculine pseudonymous persona that masked her feminine identity, Krestovsky, was no more than a fictional construct, factually "no one" as well. Khvoshchinskaya's use of the term "no one," then, not only describes her own identity in relationship to the dominant literary establishment, but also wryly reveals the identity of her listeners—other outsiders, and especially other women.

Exhibiting a humorous and spirited prose style, unusual imagination, and talent for lively dialogue, Khvoshchinskaya's prose richly deserves to be salvaged from the past. The sharp analytical skill and masterful observation of psychological detail apparent in her best work provide thoughtful and insightful reading. Richly augmenting the established body of work produced by her better-known masculine contemporaries, her vibrant prose fiction offers a fresh glimpse at the conditions of women's lives in nineteenth-century Russia. While her works retain their freshness and vitality for contemporary readers, her innovative use of literary language and her radical approach to familiar themes, such as the education of women, offer new perspectives for exploring Russian literature.

A Note on the Translation

The Boarding-School Girl was first published in *Notes of the Fatherland* in 1861. The novella was included in volume 8 of Khvoshchinskaya's eight-volume *Novels and Novellas (Romany i povesti)* (St. Petersburg: Izd. tip. Glazunova, 1859-1866) and reprinted in volume 1 of her *Novellas (Povesti)* (St. Petersburg: Izd. knizhnogo magazina "Novogo vremeni," 1880). The novella was included in volume 2 of her *Collected Works (Sobranie sochinenii)* (St. Petersburg: A. S. Suvorin, 1892; 2d ed., 1898) and in her six-volume *Complete Collected Works (Polnoe sobranie sochinenii)* (St. Petersburg: Kaspari, 1912-1913). More recently, the novella has been reprinted in the single-volume collection of her *Novellas and Stories (Povesti i rasskazy)* (Moscow: Khudozhestvennaya literatura, 1963) and her *Novellas and Stories (Povesti i rasskazy)* (Moscow: Moskovskii rabochii, 1984). The present translation is based on the text that appeared in the 1892 edition of Khvoshchinskaya's collected works.

I adopted a modified version of the transliteration system used in the *Oxford Slavonic Papers,* omitting hard and soft signs and retaining conventional English spellings whenever possible. As an added exception, I adopted the name "Lolenka" to further facilitate pronunciation for English speakers unfamiliar with Russian. In so doing, however, the name loses the visual repetition in Russian of the letter "e" ("Lelen'ka"), as well as the harmonious simplicity of uniformity in transliteration. I retained gendered endings for personal names (for example, the feminine "Khmelevskaya," and the masculine "Koshansky") and created a plural nongendered name form in imitation of the Russian ("Khmelevskys").

The Boarding-School Girl

At about six o'clock in the evening, in the beginning of May, two young men were strolling through the garden surrounding one of the homes in the city of N.[1] It was a very lovely evening. The garden, though not large, was overgrown. The friends followed a single path for a long time, often brushing their heads on the overhanging branches of a lilac bush. One of them was a guest; refined and elegant, his suit bore the stamp of Petersburg and seemed strange amid the unkempt wasteland, which might otherwise be called a provincial garden. The young man was not bad-looking, carried himself decorously upright; fine black sideburns gave him an even more earnest appearance. He wore a hat and did not remove his gloves. His host was shorter, blond; he wore an old gray coat without a cap. Although he was the younger of the two, he appeared to be the same age as his guest. His features were very handsome but seemed somehow crumpled; his complexion wasn't pale; but his sickly, imbalanced, impatient step completed the impression of dissimilarity to his guest. The guest's name was Ibrayev; he had just recently arrived in the city of N. to assume a very distinguished position. His host was named Veretitsyn; he had held a position in N. for more than a year, though a very undistinguished one. They both had been well educated, though not together, had met a long time ago, and this evening they were meeting each other for the first time in three years.

Ibrayev explained how he had obtained his position, recounted the details, and, it seemed, multiplied them to prolong a conversation that suggested no other topic for him besides this. Veretitsyn listened, attentively, it seemed, but without participating. Each fulfilled his responsibility scrupulously, celebrating their meeting after a long separation with questions and stories.

"Are you tired of walking?" asked Veretitsyn when the other had fallen silent.

Ibrayev had been tired for a long time but hadn't said so, either out of courtesy or because he had lost all hope of finding a place to sit down in this garden.

"No . . . yes. . . . But then, it's hot in the house," he said, thinking about the cramped room in which, only half an hour ago, he had found his friend.

Veretitsyn guessed his thought.

"Sit down over here," he said, leading him out from under the lilacs into a small clearing where a simple wooden bench stood. Hops had been planted around it and rose high on poles; goosefoot and bindweed sprawled in profusion along the ground.

"Sit closer to the center," Veretitsyn added, "the legs bend outward."

"Would you like one?" asked Ibrayev, reaching for his cigars.

"I don't smoke."

"Since when? You used to like smoking."

"I gave it up."

Ibrayev lit a cigar; Veretitsyn whipped the grass with a thin branch broken off one of the lilac bushes; both were silent. This was one of those moments when everything just heard or seen is vividly remembered and contemplated. The distant past is recalled and compared with the present; the tension and coldness of the first meeting pass. It becomes possible to recognize the person from the past in the stranger with whom, it seemed, there was now nothing to discuss; asking questions seemed awkward. . . . Ibrayev looked at the bent head of his friend; he remembered the blue cap band over this hair; those last empty, brief words had stirred something distant in his soul. It seemed somehow shameful to be conducting a casual conversation. . . .

"Well, what about you, Sasha?" asked Ibrayev, no longer in the soft, even voice with which he had recounted his successes in society and his career.

"What about me? Oh, nothing," answered Veretitsyn, looking around, under the influence of the same pensive mood. "I'll be living here another year. You were fortunate. . . . Well, at first it wasn't bad even for me. Of course, it hasn't been the same for you, the fortunate ones. As soon as you graduated, you were able to get established, something we, the ordinary people, never even dreamed about."

"What did you graduate with? A master's degree?"

"With honors, my friend. I was a teacher in Moscow for two years and then was sent here."

"Also as a teacher?"

"As a copyist for the provincial administration," Veretitsyn replied. "I'm under police surveillance," he added, noticing his friend's slight embarrassment and beginning to laugh.

"I didn't know," Ibrayev said.

"It's too bad that you didn't make inquiries. My friendship isn't very flattering, especially for an important person like yourself. Don't take offense. I know you're a nice fellow, but my reputation is ruined and there's nothing connecting you and me. You've already been here a whole month—I've known this and haven't visited you. If we hadn't met by accident, you hadn't come yourself . . ."

"Aren't you ashamed?"

"There's nothing for me to be ashamed about," rejoined Veretitsyn seriously. "Why would you need me? You're a member of high society. By now mothers are trying to snare you for their daughters; girls are pining for you. You're a reputable man; our 'authorities' treat you with respect. What do you have in common with an insignificant mite useful to the world merely for copying documents and nothing more? You write letters of protest, while I dare not strike out even a comma. You're the czar's all-seeing eye, but I'm a certified example of a 'harmful trend!' Where would my conscience be if I began to impose myself on you? We've gone in such different directions, we'll never meet. . . . Well, then, good-bye!"

"You're bitter," said Ibrayev, and fell silent.

They were both silent for a few minutes. Veretitsyn began whipping the goosefoot again, smiling derisively and as though in anticipation.

"Why don't you ask how this happened to me?" he asked finally.

"Oh, yes! Really, how did it?" asked Ibrayev.

Veretitsyn burst out in loud laughter.

"Oh, I don't even know myself," he answered, throwing away the stick he had been playing with. "Have you rented the apartment for the year? . . . It's too bad: that house is cold."

"Really? That's annoying. . . . And do you live with your sister?" asked Ibrayev.

"Yes, at my brother-in-law's."

"Are they good people?"

"Yes. . . . There are no bad people. Evil is only an abstract concept; it doesn't exist in reality. People only talk that way about it to have something to say. Everything in the world is fine; people are all good. . . . Sometimes they're naughty. . . . Well, there's the courts for them. Now, important gentlemen like you, for example—"

"Listen, Sasha," interrupted Ibrayev, who had begun to feel a little ashamed, "I'm still not such an important man that you can't talk to me. Do me a favor, be frank."

"Well then, I'll be frank. . . . I'm bored," Veretitsyn said suddenly, no longer restraining himself, perhaps because he was unable to do so or because his old friend's voice had moved him to speak his mind. "My brother-in-law's a clerk; he was poor, but he's got a fortune now. My sister was a poor girl; she never cooked a dinner only because she was considered a 'lady,' now a great lady in velvet and feathers—with a horde of children. Look, they're flying a kite in the yard."

Ibrayev had heard the shouts and even a scuffle in the yard a long time ago; he grimaced.

"Of course, I could go over and intervene, quiet them down," continued Veretitsyn, "but I'm no authority. My brother-in-law, their father, practiced this skill up to his seventeenth year of life, and now he's a provincial treasurer; I passed the university entrance exams when I was seventeen, and what am I?"

"What exactly are you doing? Are you studying, reading?"

"There's never any time, nowhere to go, nothing to do. I'm obliged to be at my job every day; you've seen my home: I have no books."

"But, the day is long, what about after work?"

"I sleep. I loaf around here. . . ."

"But, how can that be?"

"Oh, you public figures!" interrupted Veretitsyn. "Well, find me some pursuit, tell me what I could do. But then, isn't it reasonable to presume that such a thing doesn't exist; it's only what's called 'spinning your wheels'? Write articles, you say, since I've taught history and statistics? You still need free time for that, and the means. . . . Well, all right, suppose I found those somehow, if you will. What's there to research? You won't find monuments, historical sites, or documents around here. Peresvet's[2] walking stick was in one of the monasteries, a huge staff, two and a half yards long, and the monks whacked it in half with an ax: it didn't fit into the niche in the new church. . . . There you have it, and it's always the same. Statistics. . . . That subject's been officially treated tens of thousands of times, but try touching on something unofficial, some vital and afflicted aspect. . . . I humbly thank you! They'd send me farther away, but it's bad enough for me here!"

"These are all excuses. Listen, this is just a lack of willpower. . . ."

"Say also a lack of selflessness! What else? Really, I like you, you fortunate ones! You have no concept of real work, although you command others to work. Don't worry, we'll work as long as our strength permits, without your command. We'll work more than you, although it looks like we're only sleeping and wandering among the brambles. We think, we preserve sorrow and the bitter taste of ideas—from which good comes—while for you it's only the job, whatever that job might be, without even giving it a thought, as long as it's a job! If something obstructs your path, if some little thing doesn't go your way, you start shouting about lofty aspirations and human injustice. You smash it, strike it down—and you're right. But if one of us, the little people, can't break down walls with his head, well then, in your opinion, he's an idler, lacking both willpower and selflessness. . . . Everything, you say, is possible. What exactly is possible? You won't find a job for me, and even if you did, I couldn't do whatever it was since no one here wants to help someone like me. You're used to judging difficulties from the height of your grandeur. Do me a favor, look a little lower! . . . From your point of view, for example, there's society here. From my point of view, it doesn't exist. I don't visit my fellow copyists, and your circle won't accept me."

Ibrayev did not respond to this, but after a brief silence he suddenly asked: "But don't you at least have friends?"

"Yes, I meet people; we exchange greetings."

"Why don't you visit anyone? I've been here for a month and haven't met you anywhere."

"I don't visit the homes of those I can't receive in my own home," Veretitsyn rejoined. "However, I know everyone here, both old and young, even the ladies. Last fall and winter I was overcome by boredom. I joined the Nobles' Assembly,³ went there to read journals, sometimes even to look in on the dances."

"Did you dance?"

"With whom? I don't approach my sister's friends. I'm not introduced to others. Your czarina, Madame la Princesse,⁴ took an interest in me. You see, she's constantly thinking of all those formal social occasions with their changes of clothing and the charity performances. She saw me—a new face. She ordered my immediate supervisor to introduce me to her and enquired whether I had any talents—did I sing, did I at least play the *gudok*,⁵ did I have any recitation abilities? I had none of these, but even if I were illiterate, I would always be suitable in roles without speaking parts; fortunately, inviting me would be 'embarrassing.' I limited the conversation to an exchange of greetings since, anyway, I'd been introduced to this lady. Then, I was told that she didn't have anything more to talk about; everything had been discussed. She delivers monologues about me to her little circle and has named me *le jeune malheureux*.⁶ I became incensed. This was impossibly stupid. I stopped going to the dances. Besides, they were beyond my means: gloves are expensive."

"Listen," Ibrayev said hesitantly, "and your means, how are they?"

"I'm penniless, of course. What remained of the savings from a teacher's salary, and what my deceased uncle gave me when I graduated, I contributed to the 'household' to avoid living on charity! Well, even here I get a salary—as much as six rubles a month. They say this is very good. . . . And what more do I need! I'd consider myself God knows what kind of fortunate fellow if I had the chance to rent some attic and live by myself. Apparently, I really don't need anything more. I've grown accustomed to limiting myself, never becoming used to anything, being unaccustomed to everything, putting up with anything. . . . You know, in order to join and frequent the Assembly last winter I gave lessons."

"Well now," said Ibrayev, "splendid! I would think that occupation must be profitable."

"Yes. I taught reading and writing French for ten kopecks an hour, ten hours a week. It was very interesting and very profitable. I would have continued, but I became ill early in the spring, was in bed for six weeks, and still haven't completely recovered. . . . In short, I'm really enjoying myself!" concluded Veretitsyn, hugging his knees and rocking back and forth without looking at his friend.

"But, is there really nothing, absolutely nothing gratifying in your life?" asked Ibrayev.

"So what exactly is gratifying? Falling in love? I have, my friend, lordly ways. If I love something, it's the best. The best is very rare, and even if it's encountered, it isn't meant for us. However, I don't deny myself the pleasure . . . maybe, of playing the fool."

"Ah, Sasha, that's not good!" said Ibrayev, looking at him and finding nothing more genuine to say.

"What is good?" rejoined Veretitsyn.

"There's a lot of good in the world, but either it's elusive, people don't see it, or they spoil it themselves. . . ."

"In which category should I be included—the unfortunate, the fools, or the scoundrels?" Veretitsyn asked calmly after listening diligently.

"You're too harsh, you're bitter," continued Ibrayev without replying. "Your own failures prevent you from looking at things impartially. You must agree. . . . Don't take offense! You must agree that there's a lot of egotism in your feelings; and for people who don't know you well, this egotism might even seem like, well, simply . . . small-minded envy. . . ."

Ibrayev prudently stopped.

"Go on, go on!" Veretitsyn said calmly. "You see, I'm not offended."

"Not offended? Just this one response . . ."

"All right. What should my response be? Are you really the first to preach this to me? You speak politely, others have spoken impolitely. You try to reason with me, others have simply driven me away. You offer condolences, others despise me. I'm accustomed to everything and can listen to anything without even being surprised. I know I'm ridiculous, a lost soul living off the bread of his dear brother-in-law, the provincial treasurer; but I see nowhere, in no one, in nothing, a well-being I would envy. . . . Unfortunately for me, I've apparently talked about it in too much detail, but then, I wouldn't want to lecture anyone like that for any kind of well-being, as if people are egotists when they're insulted, as if they're blind and don't see their own happiness when it's just that life has been too much for them. . . . If there's something I could never tolerate, it's the various sickly-sweet or wise and ready maxims that people so easily build their lives upon. . . ."

"But easily, and they build—" rejoined Ibrayev.

"You're certainly not an egotist in the slightest!" interrupted Veretitsyn, starting to laugh. "Yes, it's easy, yes, they build; but the sickly-sweet or wise maxim which one person uses to build, always crushes or injures another person somewhere else. . . . But do you know, if you start thinking about this, you won't sleep very well?" Of course peace is a prime blessing . . . well, to hell with it!"

Ibrayev finished smoking, threw away his cigar, and, taking advantage of the fact that his friend had turned away, glanced at his watch. Veretitsyn noticed this.

"What time is it?" he asked indifferently.

"Seven."

"Do you have to hurry off somewhere?"

"No, it's still early," answered Ibrayev, embarrassed. "A glorious evening!" he added, looking around.

Veretitsyn looked also, but higher, into a gap where a young maple stood, concealing the sun. Its broad leaves fell heavily and turned dark, while clusters of yellow green blossoms shone as though lacquered. Veretitsyn nodded his head and softly tapped the fingers of one hand with the other, as though in time to a song running through his mind. Suddenly he clapped his hands loudly and, with this sudden unexpected sound, raised a cloud of sparrows that were about to perch in the maple tree and hops, and they now circled about the garden, not finding a place to settle down.

"What did you do that for?" asked Ibrayev, laughing.

"No reason! What's wrong with them! It's too early to be sleeping."

"Who are your neighbors?" continued Ibrayev, his eyes following the sparrows as they flew across the wattled fence into the neighboring garden.

"I don't know. There's a lot of children there. I often hear a buzzing sound when they're studying their lessons."

"Somebody is studying over there right now; do you hear? Buzzing."

Veretitsyn looked around. The hops concealed him, and over the fence he could see the entire path in the neighboring garden, which was equally overgrown. A young girl with a book in her hands was strolling there; after looking into the book, she would close it and in a low voice recite by heart what she had read. The names of historical figures and dates, which the girl constantly confused, and passages about valor, victories, and virtues, which she recited briskly, drifted toward the listeners. She had a good memory. She wore a dark woolen dress, evidently a school uniform; but instead of the uniform's white pelerine, she had thrown something dark and sheer around her throat; from underneath the tulle[7] her slender shoulders shone white. She seemed to be about fifteen. She was somewhat short, not very shapely, just a little plump. As she returned along the path, her face was turned toward the young men observing her. Her complexion was fresh and somewhat pale, but a lovely mother-of-pearl pale. The color of her eyes, which she raised as she whispered her lesson, was exquisite: dark brown with bluish whites, nicely shaped. Her gaze was unusually clear and direct.

"Pretty," said Ibrayev.

"And so happy!" added Veretitsyn, looking at her. "She's reciting nonsense—'Louis the Great,' 'All-benevolent Louis'[8]—and thinks she's accomplishing something!"

"What's it to you?" asked Ibrayev, laughing.

"It's annoying, stupid! She's satisfied with herself, satisfied with everyone; she believes that nonsense. . . ."

"Pedant! What's she supposed to do when they still teach from the old textbooks? Perhaps there's no one to explain it to her. . . ."

"What do I care if she knows nothing? It might even be better that way! But this satisfaction; look, it's written all over her face. She struggles, toils; it's unnatural. On an evening like this—she should just breathe, run, play with dolls; but she's got her nose in a book and she's happy!"

"How do you know? Perhaps she's not happy at all."

"But if she's not happy, she's been forced, so how's that for stupid obedience? Where's the life in her?"

"Perhaps she has no idea what life is."

"Then I'll explain it to her right now," said Veretitsyn, standing up, "so she won't think that reciting 'All-benevolent Louis' is an exalted, useful thing. She enjoys his company; well, let her get bored."

"Enough! What kind of prank is this?" asked Ibrayev, restraining him.

"Find me, please, something besides this prank," rejoined Veretitsyn. "There's absolutely nothing for me to do. However, calm down, ethical man: I won't trouble her imagination, 'improve' her. . . . That's as old as her 'Louises.'"

"But what exactly do you want?" asked Ibrayev, following him.

"I don't want her to be happy!" Veretitsyn said sharply. "Here you are sitting beside me; you're utterly miserable, while this little chit . . ."

They were already at the fence. Ibrayev moved off a bit to the side, like an earnest man, objecting but curious. Veretitsyn rested his elbows on the fence, placed his chin on his hands, and waited. The girl approached, reading, without seeing him.

"Well, is it boring to study?" he asked when she was near him.

The girl raised her eyes, started, and blushed slightly. However, she didn't run away; on the contrary, she stopped, clutched the open book tightly, and looked directly at Veretitsyn.

"On the contrary, it's fun," she answered.

Her voice was as self-assured as her gaze, her movements. Not only wasn't she flustered or embarrassed, she wasn't even surprised. After coloring lightly from the unexpected event of a strange voice suddenly sounding nearby, the girl didn't blush again but stood and waited to see what else he would say to her. This wasn't flirtatiousness. Her calm gaze didn't challenge or invite conversation; she didn't close her book.

"You're very diligent; you enjoy your studies," continued Veretitsyn, forgetting the goal of his conversation as he observed her.

"Very much."

"That's highly commendable. Even on a Sunday, on such a nice evening, you've got your nose in a book."

"I have to review my lessons."

"Are you studying at a private boarding school?"

"Yes, at Shabicheva's."[9]

"Are they strict there?"

"No," she answered, again glancing at him calmly, "but exams are coming up."

"Do you want to distinguish yourself?"

"Certainly."

"And do you hope to succeed?"

"Of course, I will succeed."

This game of question and answer and his own role seemed foolish to Veretitsyn. He bowed and, uttering the words "Excuse me," moved away from the fence. The girl glanced after him and started off along the path, returning again to her book. Ibrayev was laughing.

"So?" he said. "You were ready to introduce a young soul to misery and you didn't succeed? 'Away the enemies flee without having finished their pillaging. . . .'[10] A schoolgirl is like every other schoolgirl—it's 'yes, no' . . . she doesn't know how to be miserable!"

"She'll learn," answered Veretitsyn, who had become annoyed . . . at what, he didn't know.

One of his nieces, a girl of ten, who had evidently just been bathed and dressed in a very well-starched and very short little dress, appeared on behalf of her mother to invite the guest to tea. Ibrayev took fright. Calling on his old friend, he'd quite unexpectedly found him in trouble and intended even less, as a consequence of such a compromising friendship, to enter into intimacy with the family of the honorable treasurer. He searched for a pretext to refuse. Veretitsyn saw this and helped him.

"It's already eight o'clock," he said. "You'd intended to go somewhere. Don't be late. My rule is: Don't detain anyone."

"Oh, really, it's eight! Thanks for reminding me," Ibrayev said.

"Thank your mother, dear child. . . . When will we see each other again, Sasha?"

"When it occurs to you to visit. I won't come to see you."

"You're incorrigible!" said Ibrayev, shaking his hand with feeling, because they were parting.

Veretitsyn, laughing, opened the gate for him, gave him a nod, and returned to the garden.

Several holidays occurred in a row. Veretitsyn didn't go to work and wasn't very bored because, the day after their meeting, Ibrayev sent him a large number of books. But reading made him feel still more acutely that there was no one around to talk to and didn't even produce its full pleasure. During the course of more than a year of such an uncultured life, Veretitsyn, of course, hadn't lost his fondness for knowledge or his appreciation of beauty, though somehow he had forgotten how to experience the immediate impressions of knowledge and beauty and lose himself in them. They were already too dissimilar to other impressions in his life, which he thought about too much. It wasn't that he felt mired in his petty assignments. On the contrary, he tried hard and succeeded in enduring these assignments like a painful dream, without reflecting on them; but the work added a dull feeling of misery, a sickly weight, despair to all his sensations. Reading was just like a meeting with someone dear from whom we know we must soon part, and we're remembering this. . . . Veretitsyn was bored. Practical people, knowing him to be a capable man, would have offered some other cure for his boredom, like work and courage. They would have been right, of course, but often even these same practical people define work only by the word "something" and are almost offended when they're asked to delve more deeply and attach some kind of concrete image to this immaterial "something." Veretitsyn had heard this once more in his life from Ibrayev. As for courage, there's the kind that genuinely brave men who've been in battle frankly acknowledge, that there were moments when they could almost feel their caps move on their heads because their hair was standing up on end, just as there are people, who, really having endured a great deal, frankly admit that they themselves don't even know how they endured it—probably having been nearly unconscious. Courage doesn't exist. It's just hardheartedness or unconcern, noble and lofty unconcern, a virtue, but one consisting of childish forgetfulness and youthful impetuosity. . . . But for someone whose childhood has long ago been driven away by his knowledge of harsh reality and reflection, who constantly recalls that his youth is being wasted and destroyed for nothing, it is difficult to listen without malice and bitterness to preaching about courage from people who never needed this virtue. . . .

In appearance, of course, the most legitimately felt misery and boredom find expression in a halfhearted waste of mind and time on inactivity, the feverish waste of the heart, often on the impossible, even more often on trivialities. All of this is bad, but condemning it would be cruel.

Ibrayev was also bored, and also quite legitimately. The city of N. did not satisfy a man accustomed to the pleasures of the capital. Once, to distract himself, Ibrayev decided on an eccentricity, a long hike out of town, and, fatigued rather late in the evening, he stopped to rest along the way at Veretitsyn's house.

In the entrance hall, Ibrayev ran into two ladies who were leaving, and in the twilight he managed to notice only that one woman was old and the other was young. Veretitsyn was accompanying them, as was his sister, who was delighted with Ibrayev's visit. She welcomed him with a very loud greeting and called him by name to attract her visitors' attention. But the visitors didn't notice what important person had entered the house of the honorable treasurer's wife and left. Veretitsyn escorted Ibrayev to his room.

"Thanks for dropping by," he said, lighting a candle and opening the window that looked out onto the garden. "Thanks for remembering."

He was noticeably agitated, paler than usual. When, in a gesture of particular goodwill, he gave Ibrayev both his hands, Ibrayev noticed that these hands were cold.

"Who was visiting you?" he asked.

"Khmelevskaya and her daughter."

"Are you in love with her?" continued Ibrayev, not knowing himself whether he was joking or guessing.

"Who told you that?" Veretitsyn asked hurriedly, not embarrassed, but startled.

"I heard nothing from no one. It occurred to me just now. So?"

"Yes," answered Veretitsyn. He sat opposite his friend, placed his forearms and elbows on the table, and rested his head on top of them. Something had totally exhausted him. Ibrayev never took it upon himself and didn't enjoy taking it upon himself to comfort people, but the confession of a man in love seemed entertaining to him.

"So?" he repeated. "Tell me all about it."

Veretitsyn glanced around, took a cigar from his friend's open cigar box, lit it, and, feeling dulled by the smoke, having grown unaccustomed to it, said, starting to laugh: "A glorious thing, a cigar!"

"No, your story?"

"My story. . . . Have you ever been in love?"

"Never."

"Well, let this be a lesson to you. . . . However, you don't need these lessons! Do me a favor, get to know the Khmelevskys; it's possible for you, even fitting; they're respectable society. The aristocratic old lady is decrepit, true, but she's an aristocrat. She lives modestly, rarely entertains, but is well regarded. . . ."

"I know, I've heard."

"Well then, get to know her. She has two daughters: an older one, and then there's this one, Sofya Aleksandrovna . . . you'll see. They're acquainted with my sister—they condescend to this. My sister will probably mark the illustrious date on her calendar that they favored her with their company, and then you, too, after them. Get to know them. You're their equal; you're on their level. With you, perhaps, this ice of decorum and virtue would melt. . . . I haven't gotten anywhere in two years."

"So, have you been acquainted for a long time?"

"With Sofya Aleksandrovna? From Moscow. There, when the doors of respectable homes were still open to me, when fingers weren't yet pointed at me, when people didn't shun me, I would visit her relatives' home. She stayed with them for a whole year; they wouldn't let her return home to her mother. But then, to part with Sofya quickly is impossible. Such a being is bestowed on the world at rare, particularly charitable moments. Beautiful, kind as a child, she thinks and feels for everyone; gentle, she responds to any idea, sheds a tear for any suffering. . . . Often I would simply lose my temper. How do others dare speak to her, look at her? Do they understand what they're doing? How can it even enter their minds to address her like any other girl, with compliments and courtesies? Is she really like the others? To love her. . . . First, you have to understand how she should be loved! You have to offer perfection to the perfect! We had become accustomed to the burdens we carry upon our shoulders. We wallowed in mediocrity; we don't understand how great is the height above us; we approach it without thinking . . . just like old women through habit go to church! . . .

She wouldn't drive anyone away, of course, but then you have to understand how good she is, how afraid she is of offending. . . ."

"So, she's had many . . ." Ibrayev wanted to say "admirers" but restrained and corrected himself: "So, she hasn't found anyone, she's never been in love?"

"Imagine my happiness—no one!" answered Veretitsyn. "I was jealous, I observed, finally, like a madman, I decided to ask her myself. I was a close acquaintance, with nearly the rights of a friend. I talked myself into it and asked her. She's always sincere—'there's no one.' . . ."

"Well then, what were you waiting for? You could've declared yourself."

"Declare myself, then? But listen: 'no one,' and therefore, not me, either? I said to myself, Wait, she'll come to love you. It even seemed good to wait, to see her often. This frank talk brought us even closer. I myself became more frank in everything; I let her get to know me better; I was losing my mind and coldly considered. . . . You can't understand how this happens!"

"I can't, I can't. Well then, I'm learning."

"Learn! . . . You don't know what fated love is. It's not the first, never the first—so it happened to me—but then, one like this, when you tell yourself that you've found everything in this woman, everything the soul desired, when you see how life has been lit up . . ."

Veretitsyn threw away the cigar he had extinguished and relit a dozen times.

"Well, so then?" Ibrayev said.

"Well, a few months later I was sent here from Moscow—that's all. I didn't even manage to say good bye to her."

"And you met here?"

"I decided. . . . You'll understand this. When I arrived here I was deathly miserable—nowhere to go—my home . . . well, you can see for yourself! I found out that her mother visits my sister, and once when she was here, I decided to appear. She invited me to visit. 'You know my Sonechka.' You see, that gave me the right! Her mother adores her Sonechka. Sofya still hadn't arrived: she was visiting Moscow all that time; but even without her I enjoyed being at their home. A kind old woman, the other daughter—a nice girl; people you can talk to. I started visiting them often. But—either you know me or you don't—what's the difference, it soon became difficult for me to go there. For someone like me, in a false position, it wouldn't be easy anywhere. They, the Khmelevskys, knew my history, they knew I was right; they understood this clearly, but women!—so timidly, as if even among themselves they were afraid to say out loud that I was right. . . . But why talk only about the women! Men do the same thing. Well, this was painful for me: these glances, especially when strangers visited; they would encounter me, stare at me, as though wondering why I was there. My friendship was compromising; I, especially, out of the whole city, only visited the Khmelevskys. . . . I decided that I shouldn't make them uncomfortable; I began to go less often, at times when I knew I wouldn't meet any strangers. It was as if they didn't notice, but they seemed to become friendlier; that is, they understood and indirectly thanked me. This, as I hope you will understand, can be exasperating. It even exasperated me, but I didn't stop. That was last fall; they were expecting Sofya—she finally had to come. The coaches arrive from Moscow late in the evening. Her mother couldn't meet her at the station; her sister was uncomfortable going out alone at night. They decided to send a servant to meet her on the designated day to help carry her things. I heard these instructions. I had waited more than her mother and sister. In my half-year acquaintance in her home among her family where she was loved, where she was spoken about continually, I had come to love her, it seems, even more than I had loved her before. I waited for her . . . I don't know how, with an anxious heart. There was still a whole month before her arrival. I imagined that she would come before the designated time, and for several days I loitered about alone in the waiting room as the coaches arrived, as the passengers got out, unloaded, as everyone drifted away, even the guards. They recognized me there; the clerks began to look at me and laugh. I became embarrassed; I began to meet the carriages beyond the city gates—"

"October evenings?" interrupted Ibrayev.

"Yes, twice a week, in the slush, then the frost," answered Veretitsyn with a kind of persistent derision. "Add to that, I was coughing so much I couldn't stop, that sometimes I came running from the end of the world, from a lesson, that when I returned home at ten with nothing, everyone here had already gone to bed and there wasn't even a cup of hot water to warm me up. Well, these were all trifles, nothing! I was waiting all the time. With just one thought, I drove myself to the point where freezing to death was a pleasure for me: I would assist her, Sofya, sleepy, warm, out of the coach; her pale little face would shine up at me in the lamplight, the rain, the wind, the darkness, the crush of this stupid crowd that was always there. And so, it finally happened. That day, the coach was late again. I was on duty first at the gates, then at the entrance to the station, then in the waiting room, until midnight. The Khmelevskys' servant came, left without waiting very long; most likely, he fell asleep at home and didn't come back at all. When I heard in the distance, on the platform, the driver signaling his arrival . . . you don't know what one feels at such moments!"

"I don't know; tell me."

"It's impossible to describe. I rushed around as if delirious. The horses hadn't stopped yet when I opened the door. A fat lady immediately fell into my arms and, half-asleep, cried: 'My good man, hold this little chest,' and shoved parcels at me, some pillows. I shoved all this and the lady herself onto the sidewalk. I heard Sofya's voice on the other side of the coach; she was handing something to the driver; I shoved the driver aside—"

"Well, so you helped her down? After all, wasn't the main thing to help her down?" interrupted Ibrayev.

Veretitsyn looked at him.

"Yes," he said after a moment of silence, taking up the discarded cigar and trying to light it again. "I took her things, called a covered droshky,¹ sat down with the driver, and escorted her to her mother's. They hugged each other for a whole half an hour in the front hallway, and I stood there in my wet coat, admiring them. Sofya finally regained consciousness. 'Look who brought me.' They began to thank me, invited me in to rest, to have some tea. What kind of tea is that, at midnight! But they hadn't seen each other for a whole year. I didn't dare disturb them and left; in the meantime I'd remembered that my supervisor had given me a mountain of copying to be finished by morning. This had come at an opportune moment, because I hadn't been sleeping."

"Why couldn't you sleep?"

"Probably because of the cold," answered Veretitsyn.

He leaned back in his chair and smoked, even more indifferent than his friend, who, sensitively aware that the conversation was faltering, felt awkward.

"Well, you visited them again, you saw her?" he asked, even trying to display some emotion.

"I visited them, I saw her, I am visiting her, and I see her," answered Veretitsyn.

"And she?"

"What?"

"No, but . . . just how. . . . What is your relationship to her?"

"I'm accepted as before; I try not to be boring. They're attentive to me in the highest degree. For instance, not long ago in the spring I was ill; she and her mother visited me."

"Ah, wonderful! That means a lot. . . ."

"It means exactly nothing. They even visit the garrets."[2]

"Yes, but not young men from high society."

"I'm not a young man and I'm not a member of high society," rejoined Veretitsyn more sharply than he had intended, and, for that reason, started to laugh.

"But. . . . But I would hope, if she's been well brought up, then she wouldn't let this be noticed," Ibrayev said, adopting an air of concerned interest.

Veretitsyn loudly burst out laughing.

"She's been very well brought up," he answered.

"Well, then? How was your reunion?" continued Ibrayev, becoming embarrassed and searching for words. "Has she changed?"

"She's gotten prettier," Veretitsyn said, suddenly breaking off his laughter. "Yes, do me a favor, get to know her. I assure you, you won't regret it. She's a beauty, educated, intelligent. . . . Although only a common man, I lost the right to have my own opinion, but I used to have taste. And since you bestow your favor upon me, I don't dare slander Your Honor. A pleasant home, I have the distinction of recommending it."

"You're joking," interrupted Ibrayev seriously. "Maybe, to give you pleasure, to take a look, I'll make a visit, once or twice; but I really don't have time for more. And you must agree that my position in the Khmelevskys' home would be awkward, more unpleasant than yours. Marriage, at least to Mademoiselle Sophie, is not my intention, even if she was a thousand times more beautiful. I hope you won't reproach me or suspect me of calculation, but you know yourself that the Khmelevskys don't have a fortune, and I need one. However you look at it, whatever you may preach, you can't live without money. But if I only appear in their home and even visit more often . . . it's not just the talk—I prepared myself for that provincial foolishness beforehand—but they themselves, the old woman, the daughters, will simply try to catch me for a husband. Mademoiselle Sophie may be intelligent and visit the garrets, but she wouldn't be opposed, of course, to an advantageous match. What do you think?"

"Well, of course," Veretitsyn drawled, "but I've just thought of something else. It's eleven o'clock and the dogs are being let out all over; if Your Honor stays much longer they'll tear your coattails off and perhaps even get at your legs. With your rank, this adventure would be more disagreeable than for us, the copyists."

"You are mischievous!" Ibrayev said, laughing and standing up, after gathering up his coat.

It was hanging with sleeves dangling, but Veretitsyn didn't stand up and didn't help his friend.

"Well, good-bye," Ibrayev said, rearranging it himself. "Do you want another cigar?"

"Thanks, I haven't finished this one."

"So that's what getting out of the habit means!"

"Yes."

"Don't get any more used to it. Well! . . . Nonsense! . . . What a magnificent evening! You're probably going out to meditate in your . . ."

"Vegetable garden. No, I want to sleep."

"Yes, by the way, how's your garden friend?"

"I don't know, I haven't seen her again."

"Good-bye."

Ibrayev left.

The residents of N. spent the evenings of this particular summer very pleasantly. The commander of the regiment stationed in the city lent his musicians for performances in the city gardens twice a week from six until ten o'clock. The gardens came to life, becoming so crowded that it was impossible to walk through them. Fashionable stores sold an incredible quantity of hats, cloaks, and other attire and blessed the regiment and its leader's goodwill toward the elders of the Nobles' Assembly, who had moved the club for the summer to a small building with a balcony overlooking the gardens. The orchestra was positioned on the lawn in front of the balcony. Aristocratic ladies, tired of strolling among the crowd, positioned themselves on benches around the balcony, and gentlemen who had finished or not yet begun their card games in the club, came out to converse with them. The rest of the population dotted the paths; it was even rumored that the floor in the only large pavilion would be repaired and dances would be organized. Although these summer entertainments had begun rather early, in mid-May, the public had not cooled toward them; and it could be predicted that it wouldn't cool before fall if the good weather and the amicability of the civil and military leadership continued.

Almost alone among all of N.'s young people, Veretitsyn never visited the gardens. He heard from a distance, from his vegetable

garden, the orchestra's horns and kettledrums. At first these frag-
mentary sounds agitated him annoyingly, as something extraneous,
something remembered, arising needlessly to disturb the silence
that the young man had been trying to accept and to which he had
almost grown accustomed. There's nothing more annoying than
noise without people. There were enough people around, perhaps,
but for Veretitsyn they didn't exist. When night fell, sitting on his
rickety bench under the hops, Veretitsyn began to take pleasure in
the dying down of every motion and whisper, in the chilly waning
light. His emotions also became tranquil, without excess; the past
somehow receded still further; sadness felt neither dulled nor re-
signed, but profound and serene to the point of solemnity. This was
his comfort, his pleasure. And suddenly this pleasure was being
disturbed by a ridiculous crashing and thundering in the distance,
a crashing and thundering for the amusement of people who,
having done nothing their whole lives, had decided to vary their
idleness.

The music began to anger Veretitsyn when, sounding for the
first time, it drove him from the garden. The next time he almost
turned to leave, but changed his mind: it was a shame to lose the
evening. The third time he began to listen. The orchestra was playing the finale from *Lucia;*[1] Veretitsyn recognized it from a few notes
carried by the wind. He couldn't identify the feeling that made him
sit upright on the bench and, with his heart almost pounding, wait
for another fragment. He may not have wanted to be there, in the
gardens with the orchestra, but he wouldn't have exchanged the
sensations that seized his soul at these moments for anything. The
shadowy trees, the dew darkening the path, the chirring of the
grasshoppers during pauses in the melody, the pale, barely visible
stars in the depthless blue hollows between the white clouds, the
lights in his neighbor's windows, small, but bright, with trembling
pink rays, the emptiness all around, and the painful feeling in his

chest—all this was good together, it went hand in hand. A stray dog ran in through the poorly latched gate. Veretitsyn asked for a piece of bread at the kitchen window, returned to the bench, fed the dog, and listened to *Lucia*.

His mood, of course, didn't recur. The next evening he again raised his head, listening to the horns, but they burst into a waltz; waltzes and polkas continued all evening. This was more suitable to the public's taste. Veretitsyn found that listening was stupid, childish, all the more so because the children in the neighboring garden were also listening. He walked up to the fence and glanced over mechanically.

The children who had been playing in the bushes didn't notice Veretitsyn, but the young girl whose acquaintance he had decided to make a week ago saw him. Their glances met. Veretitsyn bowed to her. The girl seemed puzzled but calmly returned his greeting.

However, her calmness was more superficial this time. True, she didn't run away, didn't turn away, didn't lower her eyes; but the fixed gaze directed toward her made her feel uncomfortable. It made her feel uncomfortable to be tossing a ball with a boy younger than she—a pursuit she had been enjoying very much until that moment. She tossed the ball onto the grass and said, "That's enough, Kolya. I'm tired; I don't want to play anymore."

Kolya became indignant that his ball had been tossed away and began looking for it. The girl glanced in Veretitsyn's direction and, seeing that he was still looking at her, became noticeably embarrassed. She moved away from the children. Evidently she felt uncomfortable staying where she was, but as she moved away, she had to pass the fence, near Veretitsyn. Noticing this, she hurried to pass by more quickly.

He felt like laughing.

"Why aren't you taking a walk in the city gardens?" he asked when she had come up alongside him.

She blushed and stopped. Veretitsyn repeated the question.

"I just don't want to," she answered.

"Is it really that you don't want to? Of course, you're not free to do as you please. They probably didn't let you or wouldn't take you with them."

"Who's that?" she asked, somewhat offended.

"I don't know, whoever; your mama, your papa. They most likely went out and left you at home."

She wanted to leave but didn't, and replied, "I have to stay with the children."

"How boring!"

"It's more boring there," she rejoined.

"Who said?"

"No one said it! . . . I just know it," she continued firmly, raising her head and looking at him. "It's crowded there; you have to be well dressed, walk with one foot in front of the other, keep quiet— that's all the pleasure there is."

"Exactly," answered Veretitsyn. "The amazing thing is: Why does everyone go there?"

"I'll still have plenty of time for strolling," she rejoined after falling silent for a moment, and no longer so decidedly.

"You will? Who told you so?"

She glanced at him, surprised.

"Who told you that you'll have time?" continued Veretitsyn. "Who can guarantee that for one day, one hour?"

"I'm not about to die," she answered, smiling.

"I'm not predicting your death, don't worry. But who can guarantee that, when they decide to invite you out, you'll still want to go?"

"Oh, I'll always want to!" she said.

"Again, that's not for sure. Just now you said that it's boring there, but after a year or two . . . a great deal of water will have passed under the bridge. You may experience sorrows before then that will change your character, and the longing to see something will pass, or a longing will come along for something better than what's being offered. It'd be better if you were given the privilege now while all this nonsense still has some value for you."

"There, you yourself say it's nonsense."

"Yes, I'm saying it, I can say it," rejoined Veretitsyn. "I've seen it, that's why I'm saying it. I know how things look before they've been examined. That's why you need to experience things before they've been examined. Close your eyes, have a good time, take advantage of everything—that's youth! But what? You're a child yourself and you have to take care of the children while your papa and mama are there listening to Lanner. . . .² They're playing Lanner's waltz 'Hoffnung Strahlen.'³ Listen—a glorious waltz! Are you studying music?"

"Yes. . . . What's this waltz called?"

"'Hoffnung Strahlen.' Do you like the name?"

"Yes. . . . What a strange name! Why is it called that?

"I don't know. Perhaps there's a story associated with it. There's a story to everything. It was some sort of fortunate time for the man—he even named his work in memory of it. It could even have been a bad time."

"Well, surely waltzes aren't composed in memory of bad times!"

"Why not? People will prance around to it just the same."

"Yes, without knowing what the music means, but if you know . . ."

"What's the difference! Does only music have the ability to remind us of sorrow? Doesn't each of us know someone's grief, and not just one person's grief, but the grief of many well? That doesn't bother us. We won't whirl around to a waltz? Well, what's the difference, we'll whirl around on the earth, we're happy; even when someone else's neck is in the noose, it's none of our business."

The girl had become thoughtful and glanced at him. Veretitsyn smiled.

"Are you studying a lot, as usual?" he asked, falling silent.

"Yes."

"For exams?"

"How did you know?"

"You said so yourself, then."

She blushed.

"Really, I envied you: so diligent! A Sunday, a magnificent evening, but you, without raising your head, memorize and memorize. Is it always that way?"

"Yes. . . . No. . . . No, you know, it's for exams. There are forty-two students in the school. . . ."

"And you—what's your ranking?"

"Me? . . . I'm ranked sixth. But I'm in the lower class. . . . So you see"—she blushed again—"my mama and papa would very much like me to skip to the higher class, win an award, move up.¹ I'm trying as hard as I can. I know it would be such a pleasure for them if I passed up everyone else. . . ."

"And then your papa and mama will buy you a straw hat with a rose, a white cloak, and they'll take you out for a walk?"

Her pretty eyes burned with indignation.

"What makes you think I care about that?" she interrupted. "How dare you laugh at me?"

"Good gracious, nothing of the kind!" Veretitsyn rejoined indifferently. "I only said that because, I suppose, it'd be so nice for your papa and mama to show off their dear daughter who has given them such pleasure. They'll do it for themselves, not for you."

She looked at him.

"For themselves," Veretitsyn repeated, "who else? Well now, you're already taking their place with the younger children; you're a teacher for them; you'll be good for them and cheerful for them:

all this for the pleasure of your papa and mama. I understand it all
so well that I'm not even handing you a compliment. You're a fine,
obedient, affectionate daughter: you're only doing your duty. Always behave that way. Always live that way. Always live entirely for
your father and mother. Grow bored when it pleases them. Wear
yourself out over a book, work, whatever is happening. Parade
yourself around when they show you off—it's their will. It's nice
for them: you're their property. You didn't ask them to be born;
you have no right to ask to live any way you want. When I mentioned the new hat I was only thinking how your mama will select it
for you according to her own taste, and I wanted to caution you so
you don't argue with her choice. It's your mama's joy—don't inter-
fere. And when they take you out in public, of course, that's so all
the papas and mamas of those classmates of yours, whom you're
passing up, will look and be punished and ask why God didn't bless
them with daughters just like you. If you meet these classmates
then, you won't let them notice that your triumph makes you feel
sorry for them. . . . What's it to you! And really, don't feel sorry.
You did your duty, you gave pleasure. . . ."

The girl was pale and didn't take her eyes off Veretitsyn as she
broke off dry twigs from the fence. He started to laugh.

"I'm joking," he said. "Study, work hard if you enjoy it. Really,
I'm joking. Forgive me. . . . Do you enjoy your studies?"

"Yes, I do," she answered.

"What do you find especially pleasant?"

"That sometimes I completely forget what's going on around
me."

"Why is that important?" asked Veretitsyn. "Are things really
that bad around you?"

"No, things are fine, but it's better this way. I take a book and
often simply lose all sense of where I am. That way, you almost escape to another world completely. . . ."

"And all this, for example, this memorizing about Louis . . ."

"Lolenka, where are you?" children's voices were heard calling. "Papa and Mama are back."

Veretitsyn had noticed, but the girl hadn't: it had gotten dark. She glanced around as though frightened and took off running.

"Good-bye, Lolenka!" Veretitsyn said after her.

She would have turned around at his parting phrase, but it had seemed impolite to her. . . .

Veretitsyn liked this amusement. When there's no goal in life, amusements that also lack a goal are especially fitting: they have something in common. Life passes as if in slumber; its amusements and sorrows should be as elusive as dreams but, in the meantime, provide their own interest. The next morning, Veretitsyn, feeling unwell, decided not to go to work, picked up a book, and went out to the garden. Opening the gate, he thought about Lolenka.

She wanted to see her "neighbor" even more. Lolenka was the daughter of one of N.'s government clerks, a gentleman of modest means. The family was enormous, the children brought up strictly. For a girl who knew only the way to her boarding school, and then only under the supervision of the housemaid who was always sent to accompany her—for the school's model student, who never dared look with anything but respect upon the faces of her teachers and therefore never knew whether they were young or old—for a young lady kept strictly in check, who even went to church only accompanied by her mother or an aged relative—it was a great event, a conversation over the fence with a young and "good-looking" neighbor. Lolenka had noticed that Veretitsyn was good-looking.

But something else had struck her: Veretitsyn spoke somehow strangely. At home with her family she of course not only had never heard anything like it, but young men never visited and were never mentioned by name there, either. Her girlfriends talked about young men at school, but what they talked about in great secrecy was also unlike Veretitsyn's conversations with her. Their secrets consisted of the pressing of a hand, compliments. Somehow Lolenka didn't like this, perhaps because it was extremely uniform. She even disliked listening to these secrets, and that was why she rarely was taken into anyone's confidence. She was a boring confidante; she didn't know how to compose and pass notes, how to conceal anything, or how to get out of trouble. You could see everything written on her face immediately. It all seemed either awkward or impossible. She felt sorry for those who were deceived, ashamed before the adults. Her excuses were all the more annoying because Lolenka was not in the least shy.

She proved it that morning, going out to the garden to review her lessons, choosing a spot not far from the fence. She was sure she wouldn't see her neighbor: he was at work from early morning; but it seemed better to sit here, closer, in the shade of a large linden tree, and, dipping into Koshansky's rhetoric,[1] she took a look from a distance, through the chinks in the fence, at how the path in the neighboring garden sparkled in the sunshine. It wasn't covered with sand or crushed gravel; probably her neighbor had trampled it down walking back and forth. Her neighbor was a very strange person. Her father once said that he'd been sent here for some reason. His sister, a treasurer's wife—how ridiculous she was! Why did his jokes seem so unpleasant?

Lolenka lowered her eyes to the book and tried to understand the explanations of metaphor, metonymy, synecdoche, and irony, but she didn't succeed at all. She thought, meanwhile, that the prettiest green, shiny little bugs could be found on artemisia bushes, and she looked over in the direction where huge bushes of artemisia were growing near the fence.

Why does he have to know what I'm learning, what I'm study-ing? Lolenka asked herself. He laughs at me; well, I'm not going to allow that. And his jokes seem so strange, not like other people's; his jokes make me feel so depressed. He must be bored here; a friend, they say, of no one. . . . But I'm his friend!

Lolenka started to laugh, threw Koshansky's rhetoric aside, lay down on the ground, tore out whole fistfuls of grass, and flung it all around her. Finally she said almost aloud, However, I have to learn it. She began reciting by heart from a special notebook, among the examples:

You speak—and half a world moves
A different image and language. . . .[2]

A gap in the fence darkened; a shadow darted along the path. Lolenka heard uneven steps, a light cough, and soft murmuring, which the one producing the sound, of course, considered to be singing.

Well, he doesn't read very diligently, Lolenka managed to think before she completely lost her courage.

But she lost courage completely, and the frightened girl hurried to pick up Koshansky's rhetoric so she could quietly make her way home before her neighbor saw her. He would probably think up something. . . .

But what would he think up? What would it be? . . . I'm studying my lesson in my own garden.

And she continued:

A different image and language,
Native of the Crimea,
Devotee of Mahomet,
Worshiper of idols, Kalmyk. . . .[3]

The last line just wouldn't come to mind for anything. Veretitsyn walked along his path, read his book, murmured his song, and didn't look around. Lolenka became bored for some reason; the sun seemed somehow annoyingly bright, the grass annoyingly thick, the linden tree annoyingly dark—everything was wrong! Capriciousness came over Lolenka, as it might a child, and for some reason she made a vow never again to come here to review her lessons.

Veretitsyn approached the fence and bowed in greeting.

"What are you studying?" he asked.

Although Lolenka had absolutely no intention of doing so, she got up and showed him the book. True, she felt a little awkward speaking; in spite of the fact that it was hot in the sun, the girl had even paled slightly and her lips had grown cold.

Veretitsyn glanced at the book and returned it to her.

"Nice!" he said.

"Are you familiar with it?" Lolenka asked.

"No, I'm not, but it's nice all the same."

"I don't understand anything."

"All the better. You'll learn it that way; you'll remember it better."

"Why?"

"Just as I said. But, if you understand it, you'll begin to think about it; you'll get mixed up—you'll memorize nothing."

"You're always laughing!" Lolenka said, and threw the book aside.

Veretitsyn had begun to laugh.

"Why did you do that?" he asked.

"I'm tired of it."

"How could you say that you love to forget yourself in reading, that life goes better for you, and I don't remember what else?" he continued, laughing. "You said all that only yesterday."

"Why are you always laughing?" Lolenka repeated.

"What's there to be bored about?" rejoined Veretitsyn, still laughing. "Well, let's talk seriously. How are your exam preparations going?"

"Just as I said. . . . I memorize, but I don't understand anything."

"That can happen to anyone."

"Did it happen to you?"

"When I was a child? Of course!"

"I'm not a child," Lolenka said softly, taking offense.

It seemed even more offensive that Veretitsyn didn't smile at this.

"It'd be better if you gave explanations instead of always making fun of everything," she continued, becoming flustered as she spoke. "You know everything."

"First, I'm not making fun. Second, I know nothing," rejoined Veretitsyn.

"Still, you were taught, weren't you?"

"As a child. Since then, I've forgotten everything."

"But afterward, what then?"

"I've learned a little bit all over again."

She looked at him thoughtfully, raising her large eyes. "It must have been very difficult for you," she remarked.

"Easier than your memorizing Koshansky," he replied, "or, then again, all about those great people with whom you then . . . last time, were walking around."

Lolenka blushed.

"That's why I was surprised," he continued, "when you said your studies transport you to another, better world. What kind of world, I thought, with various 'all-benevolent beings'? And, well, with poetry like this: 'Stealing our peas a little sparrow; / Leave us, you thief, one little spare row. . . .' Look, if you will, it's right here. . . ."

"You said you'd forgotten, that you didn't know it," rejoined Lolenka with annoyance, not giving the book to him.

"You recall such amazing things against your will," Veretitsyn said, beginning to laugh. "Forgive me, however, you don't like jokes. As far as I can discern, you're a serious person; you're bustling about learning something. Perhaps even that's useful for something." He pointed at the unfortunate rhetoric book.

"In fact, I learned this at one time. I saw how others did it. I still don't see how it could be good for anything, but then I could be mistaken. Boredom itself is a useful thing: you become dull and quiet—that's good. There's a maxim that says: 'Be meek, quiet, modest, and speak less. . . .'[5] I don't remember the rest, but the moral is excellent, soothing; everything's peace and tranquillity. . . . You're memorizing nonsense; don't disdain it—that's the way it has to be! In another of your books it's written that so-and-so was a great man—believe it! Don't dare think about anything, or you'll understand, God forbid, that one great man was a petty tyrant, another a scoundrel, a third sinless only because he had no opportunity to sin. They teach you that everyone who'd ever lived was an angel—so much the better for you. A thin haze floats about in your head instead of real concerns; don't worry, even that will soon pass. You're enriching yourself with knowledge to please your parents, but as soon as you've fulfilled this responsibility, pleased them, you'll be free to forget everything you've learned. Whatever you've memorized there, why make a fuss about it? It's all suitable for now; after all, it won't be for long."

Lolenka plucked at the corners of her book and was silent. Veretitsyn fell silent also; resting his chin on the fence, he looked at the girl. She suddenly glanced over at him.

"So, I'm studying nonsense?" she asked in a rather sharp tone that made her voice falter.

Veretitsyn began to laugh.

"I'm not saying that," he answered. "What's nonsense to me

might not seem like nonsense to others. People wrote your books; these people were thinking about something."

"But were they thinking wisely or not?" she continued.

"How do I know?" Veretitsyn rejoined, laughing. "You said yourself that you forget the whole world with these books."

Lolenka turned away and looked at the shadow of the linden tree where, for half an hour before this, she'd been studying her lesson. She felt awkward and somehow regretted what had existed a half hour ago. The shadow was already shorter; Lolenka felt as though something had been lost. The grass she'd torn out and scattered about was withering in the sun. A long blue dragonfly flashed and disappeared; Lolenka concentrated her attention to see where it flew but suddenly changed her mind and addressed Veretitsyn: "What book were you reading?"

Veretitsyn gave his book to her and took Koshansky in exchange. She surrendered it without thinking but, after glancing into his book, returned it immediately.

"I don't understand it," she said.

"It's English—Shakespeare."

Lolenka was flustered as people sometimes are, innocent in their ignorance, and to recover she said, "A writer of the late sixteenth century, right?"

"Exactly," answered Veretitsyn.

"How ancient! Besides, he wrote for the common people. . . . Of course, the queen honored him with her favor, but the language of his plays is so coarse—"

"Have you read something of his?" interrupted Veretitsyn, who had begun to feel sorry for her since she was so flustered.

"No."

"Do you want to?"

"I don't know English."

"I have, I think, a few of his works in French. I'll look around and lend you something. It'll be a translation of course, but you'll become acquainted anyway."

Lolenka blushed from fear, from joy—she herself didn't know from what. It flashed into her mind: How could she borrow a book from her neighbor, and what kind of book? What if they found out? She'd have to hide it, but she didn't know how to hide anything. . . . She wanted to refuse; meanwhile she asked: "Is it good?"

"You'll see."

"No . . . but can it be read?"

"I'm reading this one for the twentieth time."

"No . . . but perhaps it's a bad book," the girl continued, nearly breathless and blushing from confusion.

Veretitsyn felt like laughing, but she glanced at him so directly and trustingly that he restrained himself. The girl had no knowledge of bad books that corrupted the imagination; therefore she did not suspect that the young man might get the impudent idea of playing a joke and lend her a book like that; but she had heard that evil existed, and her clear gaze expressed fear of finding out about it.

Veretitsyn lingered over his answer.

"No," he said finally, "it isn't a bad book, but people behave like people in it—they're not angels, or even great people. They even behave rather badly."

Her pretty eyes grew clouded.

"Life there," continued Veretitsyn, "isn't rosy, because rosy doesn't exist. Tears are tears, animosity is animosity. There's hatred and betrayal, false friendship and stupid love—"

"Why write about it?" she interrupted.

"Why?" he rejoined with petulance, because his last words had wrenched his heart. "So people will read it and become wiser sooner."

"Become wiser," she repeated, "why?"

"Don't worry," he said. "You can't force wisdom on someone who doesn't want it. Live happily; people will cry out—you won't be listening, they'll die—you won't be looking. They're all angels, all ideals. You feel fine, and that's enough for you—well then, God bless you!"

He fell silent and looked out into the garden. Lolenka didn't leave.

"Bring me the Shakespeare," she said after a minute.

"All right, I'll look for something," he answered indifferently. "What, is this all your garden?"

"Yes."

"Do you get many cherries?"

"There were a great many blossoms this spring."

"Do you like cherries?"

"Yes, I love them," answered Lolenka with a vague desire to cry.

"Are your brothers going to school?"

"No, not yet."

Veretitsyn looked from side to side. It was almost midday, and the sun shone hotly in his eyes when he raised his head.

"It's time for me to go inside," he said, squinting and wiping his brow. "What a glorious day! What are you going to do?"

Lolenka glanced at her book, which he was still holding, but she didn't dare ask for it.

"I'm going to embroider," she replied.

"Well, good-bye. Is embroidering fun?"

"Yes . . . it's all right," she answered with some distaste, remembering her embroidery frame at that moment.

"All right?" repeated Veretitsyn, and he burst out laughing. "Most likely you're making a dickey for your mother?"

"Yes."

"Excellent! Good-bye."

At home, Veretitsyn found among his bundles a multivolume, two-columned French edition of Shakespeare's works, with a small, poor illustration at the heading of each play. The volumes were somewhat decrepit, a monument of years gone by, which had somehow survived into a much later, busier, more troubled time. Those volumes—acquired with a student's savings, the beginning of a library, the first realization of a cherished dream—more than anything else reminded him of all the failures, all the useless expenditure of life, all his unrealizable, joyful hopes. Somehow they expressed more clearly than anything that it all had died. Yellowed, marked along the margins with fingernail and pencil, with pages of inserted notes and attempts at translation, they seemed like a legacy from the dead, while the owner, alive, looked at them without recognizing his altered handwriting, without recognizing his own soul in those notes.

Veretitsyn gathered them up again and shoved them into a box. He tossed only one aside: *Romeo and Juliet.*

"Here's something for her! Let her be enlightened!" he said, smiling to himself, and with this forced joke he returned to the reality he'd been summoned away from for a minute.

Lolenka didn't know herself how she spent her day. She came in from the garden perplexed and actually did sit down at her embroidery frame. Her mother reminded her that exams would begin tomorrow and it would be better for her to study.

"I've learned everything by heart," answered Lolenka.

She was annoyed at someone, perhaps even her mother for reminding her of her studies, such nonsense. . . . But at the same time the little Koshansky book had remained with her neighbor. Well, she didn't need it tomorrow; but, when it was needed, she could manage to get it back from him.

The thought frightened Lolenka somehow; she felt like crying. She calmed down, mentally telling herself that she was no longer a child.

She embroidered, moving the embroidery frame away from the window since the sunlight was coming in and bothering her; there were no curtains. This fussing prevented her from any contemplation at all while she worked, and she became twice as bored as a result. Finally the girl decided to pin a large woven shawl over the window and peacefully sat down.

"It's so dark!" her mother said, coming in from the kitchen. "What's this new idea?"

"The sun was bothering my eyes," rejoined Lolenka.

"Well, such luxuries! You've curtained off the window, so you can't see anything out on the street. Just now Marina brought Kolya and Vasya inside; they'd started a ruckus out there over a game of knucklebones.[1] It's nothing to you; you wouldn't look up even if your brothers were biting off each other's noses; you wouldn't intervene. You're supposed to be grown up, the eldest, they say! Well, they're teaching you French, but you don't want to know anything sensible. She just sits, embroiders, and puts on airs. . . ."

Lolenka was silent; the scolding continued. Her mother pulled the shawl off the window, tearing off a piece of wallpaper in the process.

"Let me," Lolenka said.

"What now?"

"It's just that the wallpaper . . ."

"You worry about all kinds of nonsense, rubbish," continued her mother, agitated; having ruined one thing, she wanted to ruin something else. "You caused the trouble yourself and then you cry over it! A lot of good you'll do sewing in the dark! There, look where your design has gone: crooked, sideways. . . ."

At this moment her papa returned from work. He had received a reprimand; consequently he was angry and shouting at the maid even from the front steps.

The children were called in from the garden, the yard, the street, and dinner was served. For some reason it seemed to Lolenka, when she sat down at the table amid the bustle and noise, that all this was happening for the first time in her life; strangely, this didn't upset her so much as surprise her. It all seemed like a dream. Very likely this was written on her face, because Papa commented: "Who beat you?"

Kolya and Vasya, remembering their fight over the knucklebones, fought over a chicken leg served with noodles and were beaten on the spot. The maid, fearing an uproar, stepped on the tail of the kitten that was hanging around underfoot; after that, Papa shoved the kitten out the window. The animal belonged to little Masha, who started sobbing softly. Lolenka looked at her and told herself she wouldn't start crying for anything. Petya and Vasya started to tease Masha. Lolenka felt as though something grabbed her by the throat; she told them to quiet down.

"Why are you giving orders?" Papa shouted at her. "I can't even say a word to my own children!"

She shrank back. At that moment her mother placed a piece of pork in a pungent, sour sauce on her plate. Lolenka hated this dish.

"No, thank you, I don't want any," she uttered.

"Eat!" her father shouted.

He was so frightening with his bristling crest of graying hair, his unbuttoned uniform without a tie, his starched dickey with the corners of the collar standing up. The pots and a pitcher of kvass[2] began to dance about on the table so much that Lolenka lowered her eyes and ate without being aware of what she was swallowing.

"Well, it didn't kill you, did it, Miss Sophisticated?" Papa asked.

He got up from dinner before everyone else and went to take a nap. The children tore out to the yard; her mother and the maid left for the kitchen; Lolenka returned to her embroidery frame. Her mother, examining her work in the morning, had created quite a bit of disorder. It was hot in the yard, and it was only three o'clock. Lolenka sat down, inserted the needle, folded her hands on her lap, and stared in front of her. She was alone; she wanted to ponder something, and somehow nothing would come to mind! She merely asked herself, Why did everything seem so strange to her today? Why was it that things had been even more depressing before, yet she had never wanted to run away?

Her mother returned, picked up a sock, and sat down to knit at the other window, opposite Lolenka. She had to work.

"Embroider, embroider, or get a book to read," said her mother. "Don't let your eyes wander and don't doze."

However, her mother herself was dozing lightly; but then, opening the window, she looked out onto the street or, more accurately, the lane, traversed by two ravines with two rickety bridges and ending in a steep slope down to the river where the city of N. stood. The lane was lined by fences with little gardens facing out behind them; there was no pavement; in the dried mud between the ruts, grass grew thick, a large number of dogs roamed, and a large number of children played.

"Well, your papa's going to lose his job soon," her mother said suddenly without interrupting her surveillance and without turning toward her daughter. "What will we do with all of you then?"

Lolenka raised her head.

"His supervisor is really out to get him," continued her mother. "From the moment they put this new man in, your father's been saying, 'If only I'd never been born.' So what I'm saying to you, Alyona,[3] is, if you—God forbid!—don't skip to the next class, you might as well not even call me your mother. There won't already be enough nonsense to do then, without teaching you, too. I'll take you out of the boarding school. Pass, so be it, we can keep you there another year, but if not—don't get angry—you stay at home. That way, you can remain a fool."

"What am I learning at the boarding school anyway?" Lolenka suddenly wondered.

The classroom benches, the teachers, the books with the complicated words, chronological charts she could never remember, and great people who, they say, were not so great after all, rushed into her mind all at once. . . . The empty lane was no longer before her eyes, but the overgrown garden with its large lindens and elms, the wattled fence interlaced with the little white flowers of a convolvulus. . . . Lolenka was no longer listening to her mother, but her mother was no longer preoccupied with the family situation.

"Is that Pelageya Semyonovna coming this way?" she asked, leaning out the window and peering into the lane.

Lolenka was thinking about her exam tomorrow and saw Veretitsyn's face before her.

"Look, is that she?" continued her mother.

"He promised me a book. He'll probably bring it this evening," Lolenka said to herself.

"Look, is she heading this way or just passing by?" her mother was saying. "Why aren't you listening to anything? You don't want to listen, is that it? I'm speaking to you!"

Lolenka looked around.

"Go on, open the gate, and keep her away from the dog. Pelageya Semyonovna's here. The maid's gone down to the river."

But Pelageya Semyonovna, a clerk's widow and the mother of two young clerks, was already climbing the front steps, successfully avoiding the dog, which was tied up close to the gate. A minute later she was in the room and hugging her hostess.

Lolenka could not stand this guest. She was a gossip who had caused quarrels between Lolenka's mama and her friends more than once. All that, of course, quieted down after a while; everyone was reconciled and continued as before, but listening to her was terribly boring. And now, no sooner had she entered the room than she began to relate a really objectionable tale.

Why does Mama like talking to her? wondered Lolenka.

The guest addressed her as well, praised her work, called her an angel and a good seamstress. Lolenka had been so lazy all day that the praise angered her.

What a fine angel I am! she thought, flushing with annoyance.

"What a smart girl I've got," said her mama. "How hard she studies, if only you knew, French and various subjects!"

"But how difficult, I would think!" noted the guest.

"Difficult, Pelageya Semyonovna, and very expensive. It's not within our means; but we have to do it. I have one comfort—my darling daughter."

Lolenka's mother stroked her daughter's head, sighing sadly.

"Is your husband taking a nap?" asked the guest.

"Yes," answered Mama more sadly. "It's better, you know, when he's asleep."

Mama began to complain about her own sorrowful fate, to relate various incidents. It seemed to Lolenka that there was no need to repeat all this. This wasn't the first time, but never had the presence of Pelageya Semyonovna galled her so much; those stories had never seemed so grating as they did now. Why go on about how expensive everything was, how they couldn't afford to educate their daughter, meanwhile hinting at some fantastic wealth and putting on airs? Lolenka felt uncomfortable. Mama, speaking about household matters, about trifling aggravations, mentioned unkindly, in passing, her deceased mother-in-law and her husband's two living sisters who, although they'd never lived with her mama, still somehow always seemed to be interfering in something. Lolenka had never known her grandmother, but she recalled that both her aunts were extremely kind.

"Are they married?" asked the guest.

"One is, with a horde of children," answered her mother. "The other one's been widowed a year, has no children, and lives in Petersburg. That's Alyona Gavrilovna, this little Alyona's godmother."

"Why does she live in Petersburg?"

"Well, she was married to a clerk here, too. The former governor liked this clerk . . . what was his, that governor's name? He was the one before the last one . . . what's the difference! It's been ten years since they transferred that governor to Petersburg; he got an important position there and took Alyona Gavrilovna's husband with him. When her husband died, she stayed on there to live. She's used to Petersburg, she says. She's always asking me to let my Alyona visit her."

"Good gracious, what for? Does she have a lot of money to pass along?"

"You're expecting too much! The capital she got from her husband wasn't huge, but still sizable; most likely, there's not so much that she's going to part with it. If there was any hope, I might have let Alyona visit her."

"Let her snuggle up to her aunt, her godmother," the guest finished, looking at Lolenka with a kind of affection.

Lolenka blushed and continued embroidering.

"So why not? The young lady's such a beauty, but not well dressed; she's always wearing just anything. You may need something better, Mother, for strolls. . . ."

"Well, she'll pass her exams, then I'll make her a coat," answered her mother. "I've already told Vasily Gavrilych."

"Has he agreed to that?" asked the guest secretively.

"He's agreed, never mind."

Lolenka's hands trembled and everything went dark before her eyes.

"You don't have to, Mama, thank you," she uttered, "I don't want any clothes or any strolls."

"How dare you not want what your father and mother want!" exclaimed her mama. "Where did you learn to answer like that? Go— the maid's back; tell her to heat up the samovar for us."

Lolenka left, did what she'd been ordered, and, upon returning, started to put away her embroidery frame.

"What are you doing? Are you going to stop working?" asked her mother.

"Yes, I'm going out to the garden," answered Lolenka.

"She's very tired; she's accomplished so much!" continued her mother with derision. "What's wrong with you today? Of all the days, today—she won't sit still or utter one sensible word. . . ."

"Don't embarrass her," the guest interjected, since Lolenka now didn't know what to do. "Let the young lady take a stroll; we've got things to discuss."

"Is there really some secret?" asked her mama.

The guest made a mysterious gesture. Lolenka picked up a book from the small table in the corner where her notebooks and classroom belongings lay and went out.

She walked slowly, as though undecided; an irresolute mood had come over her. She knew she wasn't going out to the garden to study her lessons; she wasn't in the mood for lessons. She sensed she was doing something wrong, but she couldn't do anything else. She couldn't possibly stay in the house. Even living was impossible. . . .

The shadows had lengthened; the air was warm and somehow soft. There was still plenty of sunshine, like gold, on the trees and on the grass; such a delicate, blue sky. Behind the darkened roof of the shed, over which Kolya was crawling at this moment, raiding a jackdaw's nest, there was a large bluish cloud with a pink, coppercolored lining. This cloud cast a pink shadow on the garden path. In the neighboring garden a tall beautiful hollyhock towered behind the fence; it had probably bloomed today; she hadn't noticed it before. It was blooming so early this year! Who had planted it? The treasurer's wife didn't like flowers, but then none of them liked them, apparently. . . .

Lolenka was walking along the same straight path, imagining that it would be nice to plant flowers and tend them. She felt dizzy; the book she was carrying was tiring her arms.

Why did I put my embroidery frame away? she wondered. It really would have been better to sit and embroider.

She began to walk quickly. She felt like running or singing; at times she felt like crying. She didn't intend on going as far as the fence and kept slowing her pace. Finally she left herself no more than twenty feet; she began twirling around in circles, grew tired, and decided to sit down to rest.

No. He could still say I was waiting. . . .

The children had run into the garden and were causing a commotion. Lolenka remembered she'd been called an angel and scolded them.

Now it'll be impossible to say even a word, she thought, glancing around into the neighboring garden.

"Flowers are blooming there!" exclaimed the children, observing her motion.

In an instant Vanya was up on the fence. He leaned over and looked out, holding on to the fence post. Vasya pulled his legs, contending for the spot, but Kolya, fortifying himself more skillfully than they, grabbed the hollyhock. The branch was strong; to break it, the boy used his teeth.

"Oh, what good-for-nothing children you are!" Lolenka cried.

Kolya whipped his brothers with the hollyhock, then climbed astride and, riding off, swept the whole garden with it. Lolenka walked away from the children into a thicket in a remote corner under the cherry and apple trees and cried all evening.

Veretitsyn did not come.

The first exam was in religion. Lolenka woke up early and began to get ready. She was surprised that her mother was fussing so much as she helped her to get dressed; although it was still the same school uniform, she ironed the white sleeves and pelerine especially carefully.

Her mother repeated several times, "My little beauty, make sure you study as you should. I've spoken to your father. He'll buy you a fortepiano, and you'll play it."

Lolenka hadn't noticed that this special kindness toward her had begun the night before. But she didn't remember the night before at all and was even trying not to remember it. She felt somehow fatigued. She made three deep bows before the icon, recited the prayer Before the Beginning of Studies, and set off for school accompanied by the maid.

On the way it occurred to her that two or three weeks ago she would have been happier going to the exam.

I think I'll remember everything, she thought. I'm not afraid of anything, but I'm so bored. . . . Besides, what's there to remember? . . .

Her classmates looked at her with annoying curiosity. Lolenka was too earnest and kept her silence too stubbornly. Before the arrival of the religion teacher and headmistress, whispering and laughter resounded in the hall. Lolenka paid no attention, although she really wasn't occupied with the book open before her on the desk. She glanced around only once and thought it would be nice to be memorizing, afraid, or laughing like the others. . . . The classroom monitor rapped the desk with a ruler and ordered them to be quiet. Lolenka heard her name.

"Follow Mademoiselle Hélène Gostyeva's example; look how she behaves."

"Mademoiselle Hélène really is always exemplary!" someone said not far from her.

"Look how pomaded her hair is today!"

"She excels in everything."

"Absolutely!"

Lolenka's neighbor was bent over her desk, memorizing diligently. Her full little face was nearly pressed up against the book, and her friends could see only the white nape of her neck and her thick light brown braid. Lolenka noticed she was continually crossing herself under the desk with her plump, pink little hands.

"You still haven't learned it?" Lolenka asked her.

"No . . . I can't get this at all . . . I keep getting mixed up," answered her classmate.

"If you have to speak about it, I'll prompt you. I know all this."

This classmate was an enemy, a competitor. Before Lolenka's arrival she'd been making fun of her and long ago had vowed she wouldn't permit her to obtain honors and skip to the next class. Those who heard what Lolenka had said exchanged surprised glances. But this little commotion soon ended: the religion teacher arrived, the headmistress arrived—the exam began.

Lolenka's turn didn't come for a long time.[1] She listened distractedly to what was happening around her; without knowing why, she began to think of entirely extraneous things. It seemed to her that, at that moment, in that hall, no one liked each other. The teacher seemed to complicate the questions deliberately, lead them astray, wait joyfully for them to be wrong, and didn't rejoice at all when they answered well. The headmistress, too: she looked into their eyes with a kind of malicious expectation, scolded them when the teacher wasn't satisfied; but when he was, instead of praising them, she merely turned away, composed, as if in disdain. As for the girls, it was exactly as if they had all quarreled. Each girl's face expressed fear only for herself. Now two of the younger ones were mixing up God knows what, while the older ones only laughed. And the older ones! Just now Varenka Olkhina had been flustered to tears, and Mashenka Polosova, apparently her best friend—they were always together, sharing every secret—Mashenka could have at least blushed. . . . What did it all mean? Why did the others look at someone who gives good answers as if with annoyance? Besides, how did one insult the other by learning something better? Was it envy, or were they afraid?

"Miss Belyaeva!" the teacher pronounced.

Lolenka's neighbor stood up in her place and, while she was standing up, tugged at Lolenka's sleeve. Lolenka took this as a request for prompting, but her classmate had deceived her. She knew both the question and the text well and, in answering, began confusing things on purpose.

"What are you trying to say?" the teacher enquired, speaking gently to one of the older pupils.

"Well, I can't answer," said Mademoiselle Belyaeva. "Gostyeva is distracting me."

She pointed at Lolenka.

Lolenka had not expected such treachery and blushed as though guilty. A storm arose.

"How dare you! Please leave!" the headmistress shouted at her.

"Please answer the question yourself," said the religion teacher.

"Leave your seat right now and go to the teacher's desk!" continued the headmistress.

Lolenka got up and approached the teacher's desk. She felt befuddled, offended, frightened, but remembered the whole complicated text well and could have recited it and explained it no worse than Mademoiselle Belyaeva. It would have cost her nothing to surpass her competitor and reveal her deceitfulness, but everyone was staring at Lolenka. She thought that by now everyone would be staring and shouting at Mademoiselle Belyaeva the same way, that this would be God knows what, that this whole exam was some kind of comedy, that it wouldn't be any more pleasant or easier for her if she was proved right. . . . It all seemed to go straight to her heart. Finally, she didn't know what she thought and, answering, began to muddle everything worse than the laziest of the younger students. The teacher shook his head; the headmistress scolded her. The teacher started to give her a lecture. Her classmates were laughing; Lolenka stood in the middle of the hall. When he had finished the lecture, the teacher, forgiving at heart, added, "You'll recover; let's try another question."

"Don't ask, I don't know anything," Lolenka answered firmly and loudly to the scandal of the entire school.

She didn't know how or why she said this. The teacher gave her a zero, and she went off toward her seat accompanied by the exclamations of the headmistress. Her classmates stared at her face to see if she would cry. Lolenka was pale but didn't cry. She couldn't understand at all what was happening to her; she felt cold; something pounded in her chest. Maybe it was because she was feeling miserable or capricious, but suddenly she thought it would be funny if her grades for the entire exam were zeros, nothing but zeros. Then, Belyaeva, Polosova, and the others would be happy. If Belyaeva got a zero, her father would beat her. Lolenka's own father could give thrashings, too. It probably wasn't pleasant to be beaten. If Olenka Belyaeva went from third in the class to fifth, I don't know what her father would do to her—throw her out of the house. But then, only the four best students would be permitted to skip to the next class. So, perhaps they wouldn't advance Olenka. She'd be in trouble. . . . What do fathers care whether their daughters are educated or not? After all, do fathers only reproach their daughters about their studies?

What will Papa and Mama say when they find out what happened just now? . . . Lolenka decided to spend the whole day in the garden. . . . Well, but what's there?

There was noise all around her; everyone was standing up, reading a prayer: the exam was over. The headmistress called to her, kept her half an hour, and reprimanded her the whole time. The maid had come for Lolenka a long time ago and listened to all this as she waited in the front hallway, holding an umbrella. It was raining. Lolenka thought only that it would be impossible to go out to the garden. . . .

"Unfeeling chit!" said the headmistress as a last word.

Olenka Belyaeva walked past with eyes lowered. When Lolenka finally joined the maid in the front hallway and was putting on her old cloak, Olenka ran out there.

"Good-bye, Lolya!" she said, and embraced her warmly.

"Good-bye," Lolenka said without annoyance or any strong emotion. She just felt a little sorry about something.

On the way home, she decided she had acted well, that Olenka was a sweet girl, that it was comical and shameful to exhibit your knowledge, and that she, Lolenka, would endure everything; but it would be better for Olenka if she had never been born, if the exam didn't turn out favorably. Lolenka was only annoyed that it was raining. . . .

This glorious rain shower with sun and thunder, with huge dark storm clouds that plunged across the river, caught Veretitsyn, too, as he was walking home from work. He didn't have far to go, and while he waited out the downpour in the entryway of the administrative office building, he decided it was so nice outside that there wasn't any reason to hurry to get a roof over his head. N.'s administrative office building stood on an empty square that ended in a steep precipice overlooking the river. It seemed especially pleasant there: the meadows were turning green; the entire distant expanse gleamed. Veretitsyn set off to walk along the riverbanks. The air was warm, damp, and fragrant from the meadows; breathing had become easy and comfortable.

Veretitsyn felt peaceful, almost cheerful, something that rarely occurred. Of course this wasn't the pleasure of a clerk who had just succeeded in completing his hours of work. Veretitsyn didn't think about anything; the sensation of warmth and physical contentment plunged him into obliviousness. He completely forgot what city surrounded him, what building he'd left. Somehow he didn't even remember himself, recalled nothing, planned nothing.

Youth recalls and plans, but for Veretitsyn that had passed. Its residue could be discerned in the fact that obliviousness was not yet completely dulling, but instead produced a kind of languor. . . .

Veretitsyn had seen Sofya Khmelevskaya the evening before: he'd been at their home. These visits always cost him dearly; he was both happy and tormented, and sorting through his emotions, he could never determine which was greater, happiness or torment. Already in love, Veretitsyn fell in love still more stubbornly, giving his emotions free rein. Only during lulls in the conversation when he was looking at Sofya, busy with the others, did he begin to ponder, to tell himself that, anyway, her friendliness would result in nothing, that her beauty only excited him in vain, that such relationships never crossed over into love. . . . Besides, love never moved this way, slowly, by gradual transitions! Even if it did move slowly, well then, it was time for it to arrive, really, it was time. . . . Veretitsyn was becoming impatient. It made him feel furious with the strangers surrounding him, furious with this decorous family, something like hatred toward Sofya herself. He told himself, adding unjust pettiness to annoyance, that if somebody else was in his position, and not him, not some poor fellow they received out of condescension, they might have asked him why he was so quiet, why he looked bored, or simply what he was thinking about. They were unceremonious and frank with him, why not! He wasn't a suitor. He was even less than a friend of the family; he could be sent on errands. Why hadn't the old lady thought of that before now? But Veretitsyn met Sofya's glance, and suddenly he felt ashamed; the thread of his thoughts became so tangled that he couldn't really find an end. He felt like either running home like a guilty man or throwing himself down on his knees in front of her and saying God knows what. . . . It's good that such intentions were never realized: one of them tended to produce regret; the other was somewhat awkward before witnesses. . . .

Veretitsyn stayed, became talkative, even cheerful with all his heart. He was happy, lulled into oblivion, into the most complete obliviousness to everything, except the present moment. This present didn't even have a yesterday. Veretitsyn didn't know exactly where he was, whether he'd even been alive yesterday. When the time came to leave, he took his cap, realizing that he was leaving, but where he was going or what was beyond the threshold of this house, he couldn't comprehend, didn't know, like a lunatic. . . . Consciousness came to him at home, along with a sleepless night.

He'd been happy the day before. Finding Sofya alone, he'd spent the evening with her, and the thought that she received him alone not out of ceremony, but because it was pleasant for her, flattered him somehow. Her face always betrayed her feelings, but Veretitsyn could have guessed everything even if she'd been pretending. He remembered her features so well and their slightest change, her movements, walk, habits, that he had no need to look at her to animate her image in his memory. He looked to give himself pleasure. . . . This evening she had been unhappy; she was embroidering something, working hurriedly, and complaining to Veretitsyn that she was tired from a long day spent at work.

"And I'm tired from idleness," he said.

"Do I really do more than you?" she rejoined. "Often, I'm even ashamed; taking a few days to look around, I see only embroidery frames and visits. Reading, they say, isn't really an occupation. . . ."

"Life is boring!" Veretitsyn said.

"What can be done! If we wait, it'll get more fun."

"When?"

"Soon. When something reaches an extreme, that means it'll soon end. Everyone's so bored, they must certainly stop feeling that way soon. This is just before the end."

"Before the end of the world?"

"Of anything. But if, toward the end of the general boredom, you've driven yourself to the point where you really no longer even know how to be happy, that would be bad."

"How can you protect yourself?" Veretitsyn asked with annoyance. "While awaiting future blessings, you need, if not pleasures, then at least diversions."

She meekly endured his discourteous outburst over a lecture that she had sincerely hoped would comfort him. Veretitsyn, like a bored egotist, hadn't noticed that she herself was bored; but he had distressed her even more, never imagining that she was trying to distract him out of the goodness of her heart. Instead, he accepted it as his due; he took it and gave nothing in exchange. He merely frowned. Sofya changed the subject, started an argument interesting to Veretitsyn; although privately in perfect agreement with him, she argued with him on purpose, to give him the pleasure of having his say and convincing her. Satisfied that he, triumphant, had livened up, she supplemented his enjoyment: she opened the piano and played classical pieces that, while listening to them, you lived some other, better life. She played perfectly. Veretitsyn listened, feeling faint, loving her madly, and if Sofya had understood what was being said to her in those minutes when she was playing Mozart, she would have seen for herself that her kindness had gone too far. But her mother and sister returned toward the end of the piece, and Veretitsyn, cursing their return, found it better to leave quickly and not end this evening in the usual way—banally. He wasn't fit to conduct a coherent conversation and, by leaving, acted wisely.

In the morning he set off for work without knowing himself why. By now he was used to sitting through those five hours, without paying attention to what was going on around him, since he knew from experience that paying attention meant tormenting himself in yet a new way. He was quiet and wrote whatever they gave him, knowing from experience also that delving into the sense of what was written was yet a new torment. His supervisor was angry with someone nearby; Veretitsyn didn't know the reason and didn't listen. The supervisor, who didn't like Veretitsyn's composure, wanted to incite fear on a larger scale and made a not entirely pleasant remark about those "aristocratic learned upstarts." Veretitsyn didn't even lift his head. Stepping out onto the front steps, he rejoiced at the damp, warm air and set off to wander aimlessly. . . .

Will I ever live like a human being? he thought suddenly without any special reason while—having sat down on a bench by a church near the riverbank—he looked below him at the meadow and the water.

He felt like smoking, a habit abandoned out of frugality, and because of the cigar, he remembered Ibrayev. They had not seen each other for a long time. Veretitsyn had heard from his fellow copyists of the provincial administration that Ibrayev was a very strict supervisor. These recollections elicited from Veretitsyn a sort of bitter desire to laugh. Yesterday he had seen Ibrayev's visiting card at the Khmelevskys' home, in French with two *y*'s.[2] Sofya had said nothing about him. . . .

Two years . . . well, at least one more, thought Veretitsyn. Somehow I might at least be allowed to leave this job. If only I could be on my own again, not dependent, be with other people. . . . I wouldn't have many people around . . . but who cares! At least to have the right to drive away the disgusting ones would be good enough. . . .

A storm cloud—many had passed that day—formed again. The rain began again and drove Veretitsyn from his excursion. For a moment he thought with annoyance that it would be better to get drenched than to return home; but then he began laughing at this childish idea, stretched his tired back, which had become sore and cold, and started off, increasing his pace. There was a huge puddle at the corner of the square and the street; Veretitsyn walked around it, since he had never acquired the agility of his colleagues who knew how to jump from stone to stone. Magnificent covered droshkies harnessed to magnificent trotters passed him. Ibrayev rode home from the office, but usually later than all the other supervisors; he glanced out and recognized his friend, of course, since there was no more than two feet between them, but didn't greet him. As he approached his home, Veretitsyn met Lolenka, who was running underneath a large but torn umbrella, holding the maid's arm. Her old gray cloak had dark spots all over it from the rain; the wet ribbons of her hat had turned from pink to violet and were whipping the girl's face; her dress was tucked up. Lolenka, of course, could not be pleased with the meeting.

"Ah! my respects!" said Veretitsyn, stopping. "The path of learning is difficult, but pleasant."

"Well, move along, why don't you?" the maid shouted angrily at him. "Why pester the young lady? Mischievous, these clerks!" she grumbled, walking along farther. "We'll have to tell your father. This is the brother of the treasurer's wife. He's even trying to stop you on the street; what a place he's found. . . ."

"No, really, don't tell Papa; forget it," said Lolenka.

"Well, you're right, forget it. We already have more than enough screaming and yelling in the house without this, too."

The strongest characters submit to the influence of circumstance. Nature has an undoubted influence on mood. The rain on the street, the bustle in the house, befuddled Lolenka so much that she nearly forgot what had happened at the exam. To her mama's question "Well then, how did it go?" she replied, "All right."

Mama was satisfied with the answer, but Lolenka managed to collect her thoughts only as evening approached and, going out to the garden, considered her situation. It was chilly and gloomy. Her neighbor didn't come. Three of Lolenka's four brothers, with their primers, had been tied up to the legs of a table in the house. The fourth was seated nearby to keep them company and learn by example; and that was why nothing prevented Lolenka from spending some time thinking and taking a walk. Alone, she decided to do the same thing that her neighbor did: take a look over the fence; but to do so at her height, she had to climb onto the lowest rung of the fence. Lolenka accomplished this successfully and for a whole hour observed not only the deserted garden path, but whatever was happening farther, in her neighbors' yard. Candles had been lit in their house and twinkled, passing from one window to the next. Lolenka almost cried out when the only window adjoining the garden brightened and opened; it seemed to her that Veretitsyn had opened it. But he probably felt cold: the window closed almost at the same moment; Lolenka heard only the clatter of the window sash. A candle stood so near the panes that nothing could be discerned in the depths of the room.

I'm doing something foolish, Lolenka said to herself after jumping down and scraping her hands on the fence.

She was being called home, where supper and abuse awaited her for frittering away the time, running around. . . .

The next day Lolenka returned from the mathematics and geography exams with the same success as the day before. This time she herself didn't know how it happened. She could understand nothing and had forgotten everything she'd learned by heart. Her classmates looked at her almost in fear; they asked if someone had bewitched her. They advised her to pray very hard and promise to light a candle before an icon. Lolenka thought that maybe she was ill; she felt muddle-headed. At home, mishap after mishap occurred as if on purpose. One brother hurt himself badly, falling from the attic; another broke some dishes; her mother found some of the linen missing and fired the maid; Papa had received a reprimand, and from that point on everything got even worse. In passing he said to Lolenka, "Look here, Miss Sophisticated, I ran into Father Yevsevy today. You, he says, are learning nothing, God forbid! When I get finished with you, you're not even going to know what hit you! . . . Don't you dare talk back, either! And she's thinking about getting married. . . ."

The last words were a puzzle to Lolenka. Married? To whom? She was all of fifteen years old. . . . Surely Papa was joking.

Lolenka recalled every similar joke; they oppressed her heavy heart still more; her feverish mind understood them differently than before. The girl asked herself, What did I do to deserve all this?

Why am I "Miss Sophisticated"? I don't ask for fancy clothes; I wear what's made for me. More than once my classmates have said I was poorly dressed. It never even occurred to me to want something brand new and beautiful. I know that everything's expensive and that Papa has to support all of us; I'm thrifty. . . . What are they scolding me for? I mustn't dare talk back. . . . But the others talk back! They talk like that to me because they know me; they know that I'm not like the others—I won't talk back. . . .

Her mother, having heard about Father Yevsevy's remark, also commented: "Who'd want you, a fool, for his wife? Just you try that with me, don't get a certificate of achievement or at least some book, don't skip to the next class. As God is holy, I'll make you knead the bread instead of the maid!"

Lolenka picked up a book and tried to review, but between the lines a thought flashed through her mind: Why should I review? I know everything, and I even know what I mixed up there both yesterday and today. I don't care how I answered, good or bad: what's mine will always be mine. I'm studying for myself, not for the teacher, not for the headmistress, not for any certificate of achievement, any book, but for myself, to know. . . . Besides, what nonsense! Is this really knowledge? It's just drivel: "Pompadour, this leech of France . . ."[1] What a joke, really! Who's this Pompadour? Nothing's said—just memorize it. . . .

Lolenka flushed in anger, closed the book, and stood up. A fresh breeze, the fragrance of a linden tree, wafted in from the window.

"Where are you going?" asked her mother.

"I'm going out to the garden: it's hot," answered the girl.

"'I'm going out to the garden'! Take a book, you shameless girl! I'll give you a garden! Tomorrow I'm going to the school myself.

I'll find out what you've been doing there. We sat her down like a lady, asked nothing of her, but that's not good enough for her—she decided to be lazy. . . . Really, mark my words, Alyona, you'll be bending over a laundry tub. . . ."

Lolenka left quickly. She'd heard her father awakening from his after-dinner nap, and he always awoke angry. She became frightened.

And really, she thought, opening the gate with difficulty because her hands were trembling, they can do whatever they want with me. . . .

Completely agitated, she walked up and down the path several times. The air felt heavy over her head; her chest felt tight; several times tears started to her eyes and disappeared again. She threw the book down on the grass and uttered loudly: "What misfortune!"

She herself didn't know what she was calling misfortune—everything. The exams, the frivolousness of her studies, her papa's and mama's anger, and mainly, something inside her began to feel like misfortune. Something inside prevented her from feeling peaceful, as before. . . . With sudden resolve, she went up to the fence. After pulling herself up, she leaned over and looked across. Veretitsyn was in the garden, alone but far away. Lolenka waited a few moments, and when he turned in her direction, she shouted, "Hello!"

"Hello!" answered Veretitsyn from a distance, and walked on.

Lolenka entirely unconsciously remained where she was. Veretitsyn made a complete circuit of his garden and, arriving alongside her, looked up and laughed.

"What kind of bird is this perching here?" he asked. "Be careful, don't fall!"

He lowered his eyes again to the book he was reading. Lolenka was afraid he would leave and asked hurriedly, "Didn't you promise me a book?"

"Which one?"

"Shakespeare."

"Oh, Lolenka! I'm sorry, I forgot," he said, approaching. "How did you remember? I'd think you wouldn't have time for Shakespeare."

"Why?" she asked, growing pale when he called her by name.

"Here you are, studying so much, working so hard, taking exams. Well then, how were your grades? 'B' or 'A'?"

"I flunked," she answered, and burst out laughing.

"Modesty is an adornment of woman," Veretitsyn said seriously. "All the more so for a girl, and even more so for an exemplary daughter working hard for the pleasure of her parents. Forgive me for asking—it was out of concern."

"No, really," continued Lolenka, growing pale and laughing as her voice broke from trembling. "On two exams I confused everything—I didn't answer a single question. . . . I'm not joking. Really, I'm not being modest. . . ."

"What's wrong with you?"

"That's just it. I don't know. I didn't feel like answering; it's boring to talk about."

"Was it on a whim?"

"A whim!" she repeated, lowering her head. "I'm studying for myself. Let them give me whatever grades they want: I know what I know, and that's that."

"Yes, but you see, the teachers don't know this, especially if you mix everything up."

"Well, so what?"

"They'll put you at the bottom of the class."

"Probably," she uttered, holding back her tears.

"And how about your mama and papa?"

"I'll tell them that I know it—it's my business. . . . What are you laughing about?"

"Nothing. That's fine if your papa and mama believe you."

"I've never lied in my life. They have to believe me."

"Oh, they have to!" repeated Veretitsyn. "Your papa and mama never imagined that they'd 'have' to do anything in relation to their children. . . ."

"What did you say? I wasn't paying attention."

"Nothing. Of course, if you're so sure of your parents, then you don't have to worry—that's very fortunate. But, if I were your papa, I wouldn't tolerate such things."

Lolenka was looking into his eyes.

"I wouldn't tolerate it," repeated Veretitsyn. "Today you don't feel like taking exams, tomorrow you won't feel like getting married to whomever your father chooses. What kind of a daughter are you? What kind of a father is he that no one gives a cent about him? 'Oh, Papa, you have to believe me!' Your father fussed, labored, endured I don't know what, even to the point of humiliation. Perhaps he dissembled and sinned more than once, just to have the chance of giving his daughter an education; but she doesn't want to please him in anything—on a whim! 'I'm studying for myself!' Is she her own daughter and not her father's? So, she thinks the time will come; she'll start living for herself, not for Papa and Mama—"

"Are you making fun of me, or are you saying all this seriously?" interrupted Lolenka.

"What kind of joke is it when the whole world thinks that way!" rejoined Veretitsyn. "Have you really never heard this—well, if not from your papa and mama, then from others, and, praise God, from so many of them, too! Really, has this never been said in your presence?"

Lolenka didn't answer.

"And since everyone says it, then it must be true," continued Veretitsyn. "There's nothing to be whimsical about, nothing to ponder. Whoever decided it was necessary to live this way was wiser than we are: it's quieter for everyone. You can judge from your own experience: you'll finish your exams satisfactorily; at graduation. . . . Will there be a graduation?"

"Yes."

"At graduation, the governor will give you a certificate of achievement. The bishop will bless you; you'll kiss his hand—how nice! You'll come home. You'll be wearing a pretty white dress, scarlet ribbons; there'll be *pirog*[2] for dinner. Father and Mother will be cheerful. They won't let the children touch your certificate, so they won't get it dirty. They'll let them look from a distance—because of the gold. And for a whole week, they'll tell stories about how Lolenka distinguished herself—"

"You're talking to me as if I were a little girl," she interrupted. "I don't want any of that, awards, kindness . . . nothing!"

She had grown pale and turned away, frightened by the words that had burst from her. Veretitsyn smiled, looked at her, and waited.

"I don't want them to reward me for nonsense," she continued. "I don't want to learn nonsense. You yourself said that this is all nonsense; I don't want to know it. . . . I've thrown it away into the brambles. . . ."

"You didn't!" Veretitsyn exclaimed, laughing loudly.

"Let anyone who thinks these Pompadours are clever study about them," Lolenka said, agitated and forgetting herself. "I'm not going to offend my classmates because of such stupidities, take awards away from them. Their friendship is more precious to me than any award. . . . Let the cowards, those who are afraid, strive for these things, but I'm not afraid. Let them make me a cook, a housemaid. . . . I'm not a slave! . . ."

She suddenly started to cry and ran off. Veretitsyn stood where he was and looked after her, guessing that she wasn't going home. In fact, her pelerine stood out white in the distance, in the bushes.

Veretitsyn went to his room, picked up *Romeo and Juliet* along with Koshansky's rhetoric, which had been set aside, and returned to the fence. The children were already running around in the neighboring garden; Lolenka was wandering around as if she were trying to find a place to hide, and not looking back.

"Come here," Veretitsyn said in a low voice after waiting for the children to move farther away. "Here's the Shakespeare for you."

She walked over to him, looked into his eyes, became embarrassed at his half-mocking, half-affectionate glance, and took the thin book.

"Hide it in your pocket, fold it in four," continued Veretitsyn, "and this is yours."

She reached for Koshansky's rhetoric, blushed, and smiled.

"Don't be angry, Lolenka," Veretitsyn said. "You're still a very young girl, but a good girl just the same."

She felt embarrassed and happy for some reason; she bowed her head to hide her face from Veretitsyn; but, when she decided to look at him, he was already neither by the fence nor in the garden.

The next day was a holiday in the parish, and Lolenka's mama, to her great surprise, told her that evening that she wouldn't be going to her exams but should get up early and prepare for church. In the morning Mama ironed the ribbons and straightened Lolenka's hat. She added four rosebuds, stored for a long time in the chest of drawers, under the rim. It couldn't be said that the hat was any more beautiful as a result. It was turned up somehow, but Mama liked this very much. She then took out a light blue *peau de soie* mantilla[1] from the chest of drawers, also stored for a long time— that was why it had a few creases that couldn't be ironed out—and a pale yellow necktie that would probably look nice on Lolenka because Lolenka was a brunette. Lolenka was dressed in all this, along with the white muslin dress prepared for graduation. Anxious and fretful, Mama ordered her to make the sign of the cross and say a prayer over everything she was putting on. They took so long to get ready that the church bells had even stopped ringing. Papa hurried; he was wearing his uniform and was also going to church. Even Pelageya Semyonovna, who had arrived so they all could go to pray together, hurried and offered her advice about Lolenka's attire. They pestered her so much that Lolenka barely succeeded in hiding her neighbor's book under her mattress. A sinner, she thought throughout almost the entire service, afraid that the children had pulled the book out in her absence. The thought also occurred to her that the German exam had begun by now; yesterday the head-mistress had said they had to finish the exams quickly, today, and that was why this morning three subjects had been scheduled. Then names began spinning around inside her head, not grammatical examples, not historical names, but those that yesterday, almost in the dark, she had read, peering into that book. There was something absorbing there: duels, masks . . .

"Just like a stone statue," her mother commented to her out on the church steps. Her father was conversing with some gentlemen—apparently, Pelageya Semyonovna's sons. It occurred to Lolenka to take a look at them; but she wasn't surprised, although she might have been, that her father was speaking with young men and that three of these young men were accompanying them to the crossroads. Something about them was strange! They were talking, somehow yelping. One was playing with a cane; he poked an old woman passerby with it. Another, the one talking to Papa, was constantly taking out his watch and looking at it. They all had tightly curled hair. . . .

"Your eyes are wandering again!" whispered her mother, who was walking beside Pelageya Semyonovna in silence.

The crossroads was nearby. Pelageya Semyonovna's eldest son, the one with the cane, let the young man with the watch know by nudging him in the ribs.

"Stop it, little brother," rejoined the one occupied by his conversation with Papa, "or I'll push you into a puddle."

He laughed playfully. Papa, it seemed, liked this: he laughed, too. Lolenka felt embarrassed; she'd become bored and, for no reason, of course, was suddenly reminded of Veretitsyn's laugh, his soft, somehow full voice, his slender hands on the fence, his hair, which he always flattened so much with his cap, his dark gray eyes, and his attentive gaze. Yesterday he'd said "a good girl." How did he dare say "Lolenka"?[2]

Lolenka didn't even notice how the young men and Pelageya Semyonovna said good-bye and how Papa, Mama, and she herself arrived home. Mama told her to change her clothes and go finish her exams. It was only eleven o'clock. Lolenka was distracted by her fancy attire, that morning's variety of impressions, and the many people she had seen. It was nice to be out in the open air, walking for a while, too, though only to school. She had only a vague notion of what would occur at school. Twice she forgot which books to take with her and returned for them from the front steps, but she didn't forget *Romeo and Juliet;* she carried the book in her pocket just as Veretitsyn had instructed her. But then, she suddenly thought about dashing to her little spot in the garden for some reason. She raced there, up to the fence, and looked over. There was no one on the path, but the window overlooking the garden, the one she'd noticed before, was open. Veretitsyn was sitting at the window, writing something. The new maid called the young lady to accompany her; Mama heard, and when Lolenka was crossing the yard, Mama asked her where she'd been. Somehow unintentionally, involuntarily, Lolenka answered that she'd gone to get a pencil she'd left in the garden yesterday. She felt so distressed, so ashamed of these words, that she almost started crying along the road. Feeling remorseful, of course she could remember nothing necessary for her exams; she still managed to arrive in time for the German exam; she had to recite some poetry she'd never understood but had memorized by heart. Scarcely having arrived, scarcely having sat down in her place, not having time to collect herself, she confused the rhymes—the only thing that guided her—and then began confusing everything else. The teacher, a German, joked about it very wittily, but this new failure befuddled Lolenka even more. A Frenchman replaced the German; a history teacher replaced the Frenchman, terribly quickly, one after another. The Frenchman dictated such an example of cacography[3] concerning the *participe passé* on the blackboard that even he had difficulty figuring it out and consequently flew into a rage. The history teacher started to ask about some wars. A moment earlier, while the examiners were being changed, Lolenka looked into *Romeo and Juliet* as if consulting a textbook and found there, almost on the first page, something about the absurdity and evil of bloodshed. Next to her, her classmate Olenka Belyaeva was answering the question and reciting the names of great men.

What great men? They're villains, Lolenka decided, trusting Veretitsyn's book, thinking about Veretitsyn, about his laugh. Suddenly Louis the All-Benevolent was mentioned, and Lolenka couldn't restrain herself any longer and started to laugh loudly. A strange urge to laugh had come over her; this strange urge was followed by a reprimand, a question addressed to her, and then the stubborn, ardent, suddenly dawning conviction that this was all nonsense, good for nothing; and then everything in her mind and heart turned upside down. She began to answer, but jumbling everything. To the teacher's reproof she retorted that it was no wonder she got confused when it was so unclear in the book. And when she was told not to discuss it, but just repeat what she'd learned, she said, getting carried away, very boldly, that it wasn't even worth learning, except perhaps to forget and learn again from other books. . . . The teacher was astonished. He had been teaching for twenty-five years and had qualified for a pension, but nothing like this had ever happened to him.

This scandal concluded the exams at the boarding school. Needless to say, Mademoiselle Belyaeva passed with honors and skipped to the next class, while Lolenka remained in the lower class and dropped from fifth to fifteenth.

"You should be expelled for your insolence," the headmistress said to her.

She didn't expel her, however, because a superfluous student was still worth money. Lolenka looked into her classmates' eyes, thinking she'd find sympathy, but her classmates avoided her, not so much occupied with their own problems as—God only knew what they felt. The entire administration was against Lolenka—how did you oppose the administration? Lolenka's failure was unexpected. It was impossible that she really had forgotten everything, didn't know it; but who really knew? She had said something somewhat related to the subject, but who cared about that subject, anyway? Why send them to boarding school and teach them if it wasn't to finish the course and obtain honors?

Lolenka went home. Graduation was held two days later, and her parents learned what kind of joke she had in store for them. She had to spend some time crying, too: her mother beat her, and not just once.

These catastrophes, the noise in the house, then the silence for whole days in cramped quarters, the multitude of children, and the untidiness affected Lolenka so much that she seemed to become dull-witted. Having cried quite a bit, she suddenly stopped, out of either indifference or despair. She noticed that they treated her worse when she was crying, but her tears disappeared suddenly, without any calculation. On the contrary, she thought, even if it made her feel better, she wouldn't shed another tear. Her mother gathered a whole bundle of the children's old socks and shirts, flung them at Lolenka, and made her mend them; besides that, she was given embroidery work. Lolenka worked from matins⁴ until nightfall, getting up only for dinner, but this had become so difficult for her that she would have gladly skipped dinner, especially since she didn't eat anything. At moments, especially toward evening when the wind blew through the window and rustled through the embroidery frame, she raised her head, looking around. Something seemed to burn her eyes, and the idea of running away flashed through her mind. She spent the whole day in the sight of her father, mother, and the children: she slept in the same room with the children! There wasn't a free moment to sit peacefully and think, even at night; but at night there was never time: she fell asleep quickly and soundly. One night she felt like crying in bed for a while—the children wouldn't let her; they pestered and teased her. At first, they'd been told to tease her and not to mind her, then they continued doing so without being ordered. Once, unexpectedly, it occurred to Lolenka: What if I suddenly lose my mind?

She no longer imagined either situations or adventures—inventions that soothe grief and almost pleasantly chafe at the nerves. There was something in her stronger than all these inventions. Once her mother had said to her: "Why don't you look anyone straight in the eyes?"

Lolenka glanced at her and turned away: she felt frightened. She told herself that it was a sin tormenting her. She wanted to die. . . .

This continued for about a week. Pelageya Semyonovna dropped by for tea and found, as always, Mother at one window, Lolenka at the other.

"A real seamstress, young lady!" she commented affectionately. "So what's this, Mother, always keeping her at work? Today's Sunday; at least let her go listen to the music. . . ."

"There's nothing for her to wear to go strolling about," rejoined her mother. "There's been no decent clothes made."

"Why is that?"

"She hasn't deserved it. There, ask her about it yourself, the shameless girl, how madame praised her in front of everybody for my benefit, that there's no one worse than she, an illiterate—"

"Don't embarrass her so," interrupted the guest, stroking Lolenka's head. "You have a nice, good little daughter. Come now, who doesn't have some sin or trouble? What good are these studies, Mother? Are you and I any worse off without them? Instead, there'd be some money! Well now, little by little, you'll teach her housekeeping—you're an expert at it—and she'll also need to learn some music. . . . Do you, my beauty, know how to play some music? Maybe a waltz or some polka?"

Lolenka was silent; it felt as though Pelageya Semyonovna were still stroking her hair.

"Or a quadrille, perhaps?"

"Cat got your tongue?" exclaimed her mother. "Do you know how?"

"Yes," answered Lolenka.

"Tell another lie, like you did then!" continued her mother. "There now, when it comes time to accomplish something, you'll give us some lah-dee-dah again just like at the exam."

"Well now, my beauty, you get busy and learn," the guest intervened affectionately. "It's really impossible without it. . . . Well now, what have you been stitching? Surely, Mama dear, you'll let her take a stroll in your garden, at least, and you and I here . . . I have a little matter to discuss with you. . . ."

"Well, go on!" said Mama.

Lolenka stood up, put away her embroidery frame, and went out. Her legs felt weak at the knees; she hadn't taken even twenty steps in the house for several days.

"What little matter?" asked Mama.

"About the eligible bachelor again, my dear," answered the guest.

The eligible bachelor, Farforov the clerk, the same foppish fellow with the watch, a friend of Pelageya Semyonovna's sons, who had come to take a look at Lolenka during church and then was so "polite" with Papa, had sent Pelageya Semyonovna to ask for permission to marry Lolenka. The fop would probably get a permanent position this year: therefore it was time to think about a wife. Lolenka would turn sixteen this year: therefore it was time to marry her off. The fop was his mother's only son. The mother was a bad-tempered old woman, but ailing, and had money. Her aunt, her godmother, Alyona Gavrilovna, might bestow a little something on Alyona Vasilyevna, well then, God be praised! But he was seduced by her beauty. "'I only require music,' he says; 'it's really impossible without it.' When he gets his position, you'll give your blessing."

"It'll be flattering for her, so young, to marry such a handsome man," concluded the guest, "and you only have to write to sister Alyona Gavrilovna in Petersburg regarding a bestowal, and then the dowry. . . ."

Mama began to calculate with the guest exactly what and how much was needed for the dowry. The suitor, besides music, requested six silk dresses. Mama was almost prepared to agree to four. . . .

Because it was Sunday, the children had been turned loose into the meadow with the other neighborhood children; Lolenka was alone in her garden. Somehow she didn't rejoice at the freedom, either because she had sat so long and was weary or because her heart, like something toughened and deeply crushed, couldn't recover all at once. Lolenka walked slowly, trying only to breathe as deeply as possible. The thought didn't occur to her as usual that, Pelageya Semyonovna is unbearable, and what does Mama see in her! On the contrary, she thought, Leave them alone, it's good for them to be together. For a moment she wished that one of her classmates was with her . . . but which one? Not one of them had come to see her. They're having fun now, perhaps; perhaps they're out strolling; listen, the music is starting up in the city park. . . . And will it be like this every day?

She felt like throwing herself onto the grass and crying. She restrained herself, glancing involuntarily into the neighboring garden. Veretitsyn was standing there, resting his arms on the fence.

He'd been standing there a long time, even before Lolenka's arrival, going up to the fence and, through habit, mechanically resting his arms on top of it. His mood was gloomier than usual, as occurred when someone surrendered to reflection and gave his nerves free rein. In the distant music there was something oppressive and annoying; but music can soothe only an egotist or a child, even though this child had long ago grown to adulthood. . . .

Veretitsyn didn't even hear the rustle of Lolenka's dress and noticed her only when she noticed him.

"Why haven't I seen you for so long?" he asked, extending his hand to her.

Lolenka gave him hers without surprise, without any emotion; she only felt cold.

"I haven't had time," she answered.

"Yes! . . . Well then, how are things?"

"It's all over."

"Congratulations."

"For nothing. I've been held back with the younger students and ranked last in the class."

Veretitsyn shook his head. "Did you do this on purpose?"

"No, I don't know myself. . . . Yes, almost on purpose."

"Why?"

"You know. . . . Why talk about it! It's boring. You know better than anyone, better than I do."

"I, Lolenka?"

"Well, yes. After all, you said. . . . What you said here—you remember."

"For goodness' sakes! Whatever I said, I could've been mistaken. I could've been joking. . . ."

"You weren't joking. I kept asking you: Are you joking? You always said, No. You were telling the truth, too. . . . I could tell that. It's all true, about everything, everyone, all true! . . ."

"For example?"

She had become embarrassed. The thought of her father and mother made her purse her lips, restrain both words and tears. Veretitsyn looked into her face and repeated, smiling, "For example, what truth did I tell?"

"For one thing, that putting on airs, showing off, is bad."

"Lolenka, I never said that."

"I understood it that way," she answered very firmly, "and I even acted that way."

"Is anyone thanking you for it?" he asked. "Were you praised? Did the classmates for whom you've made such a sacrifice throw their arms around your neck? . . . What? No one?"

"Of course no one," she answered, feeling a little offended, "but I acted well."

"You have romantic ideas, Lolenka. Give the Shakespeare back to me. You've read enough—things might get even worse."

"What will?" she asked, trying to determine whether he was joking. "Oh, you're making fun!"

"I am making fun—of you. Judge for yourself. Your papa and mama must be angry, God knows how much; your friends are laughing at you; you don't know what to do. You're deathly unhappy, but you keep repeating, 'I acted well.' You're a stubborn girl—that's what!"

"Scold me some more!" she said, gazing into his eyes.

Veretitsyn smiled at her gaze and gave his hand to her again. She grasped it in both of hers. Veretitsyn took his hand back.

"How are you going to get by in the world?" he asked.

"Somehow."

"Somehow is impossible. Behaving sentimentally and willfully has unhappy and even unseemly consequences."

"How's that? Why unseemly?"

"Here's why. You know people have to coexist somehow. They're all created differently, and that's why laws, rules, proprieties, are invented to hold them together. The way one person acts in such and such a case is the way others must act without fail, otherwise everyone would tug in his own direction. What would be the result of that? You didn't like what you were taught—try something else! You didn't like living with Papa and Mama—run away! It's just as well, thank God, that such advocates are still few, and those that spring up—well, there's the courts for them. This willfulness causes disorder. Be satisfied with what you're given. And sentimentality? Why stuff your head full of ideas that you should love any of your classmates, never show off before them, and so forth? Your classmates don't do this for you, do they?"

"Well, so what?" she interrupted.

"Again!" he exclaimed. "It just won't do, my dear Lolenka! After that, you'll give up your possessions to anyone who comes along, you'll give up the person you love—and no one will thank you! . . ."

He laughed because she had started to laugh merrily, but blushing and without looking at him.

"What are you going to do?" continued Veretitsyn.

"When?"

"Well, soon, if you like, in the next few days. You won't be going to the boarding school any longer?"

"No, I'll be completely withdrawn."

"You see! You'll be sitting at an embroidery frame. . . . Do you receive guests?"

"Yes . . . some rubbish."

"Lolenka! What kind of arrogance is that? How dare you call them rubbish? Your papa and mama like them. You're the eldest daughter. You should receive them, entertain them."

Lolenka bowed her head.

"I'm not joking," continued Veretitsyn. "The guests aren't to your liking; housework probably isn't to your liking, either, is it? What exactly do you want?"

"I want nothing," she said softly. "Do me a favor, don't laugh at me."

"This is no laughing matter," Veretitsyn answered, laughing

hard. "A young girl should be modest, industrious, respectful toward her parents, satisfied with everything, careful about household expenses, courteous to strangers—and what are you?"

"I don't know. . . . I'm probably hopeless!" she answered.

"Well, don't lose hope!" he said, still laughing, but affectionately. "And don't cry, Lolenka."

"I never do such a foolish thing."

"You would have to cry sometimes, over all your other foolishness."

"You're so difficult to understand!" she rejoined, glancing at him again, then fell silent.

Veretitsyn also fell silent, after raising his head and listening to the music.

"Will you always live here?" asked Lolenka.

He glanced around. "What?"

"No, but . . . I asked. . . . What do you do all day?"

"I serve my country."

"Don't you get bored?"

"Impossible!"

"Do you know many people?"

"Well now, I know you."

She caught her breath. Veretitsyn was distracted, listening.

"I still haven't finished reading your book. When I do, will you give me another?"

"What? . . . Yes, sure."

"I'll learn everything all over again," she said shyly.

Veretitsyn was gazing into the distance. He both heard and didn't hear what Lolenka was saying. Her last questions, the sounds in the distance, the damp caressing breeze—the kind that occurred in the evening—stirred his soul. On clear evenings, there were special moments when a wasted day was remembered more

powerfully and, beyond that, other wasted days, wasted desires—
everything to which a weary heart proclaimed—as when the pale
light of a dying sunset illuminated all the work left unfinished—It's
too late!

"I'll learn everything again, just like you," Lolenka said.

"Praiseworthy intention!" answered Veretitsyn without turning toward her. "Your papa and mama will have something to argue about;
and meanwhile you'll sit, reflect about the new discoveries in
astronomy—a very useful amusement and very restful: no one will
disturb you. Guests will come; they'll begin for you: 'Did you hear that
the deacon submitted a complaint about the sexton?'[1] or, 'Oh, miss,
you have such charming eyes!' But you have the most relevant little
question for them: 'What's your opinion of President Bonaparte's coup
d'état? . . .'[2] It's all so nice, so fitting. I advise you to try it."

"You never say anything plainly."

"Then what? It'll be so easy for you, being with people who understand you so well: it's such a comfort to the heart. According to
your custom, you'll forget the whole world in a book, but then
you'll look around, and this world before you is an unkempt mon-
ster and you see that you can forget it with a book, but you can't
hide from it in a book. . . . I advise you—study. Have they called
you crazy yet?"

"What am I going to do?" asked Lolenka.

"Really, I don't know, Lolenka," he answered softly.

"You're probably very bored. Tell the truth."

"What can I do? They don't ask me to take exams."

"Stop joking all the time. How do you live?"

"As you see."

"That's not what I mean!" she rejoined impatiently.

"Well, I don't know what more you want," he answered.

They both fell silent. Veretitsyn had become pensive. Lolenka didn't leave.

"So, have you asked your papa and mama to forgive you?" he asked, glancing around and for that reason remembering her.

"Why?"

"Just because. Try it. Well now, they'll forgive you, cheer up, take you out for a stroll."

"It's better here," she answered.

Veretitsyn didn't say a word; he wasn't thinking about her. The gate to his garden rattled, and the noise of footsteps, made by elegant, extremely elegant, shoes sounded on the path. Veretitsyn looked around.

"Ibrayev, hello!" he said, and went off to meet him.

Ibrayev seemed agitated.

"I'm here just for a minute, I'm off to the club," he began as soon as they'd reached each other and exchanged greetings.

"I wouldn't dare detain you," answered Veretitsyn.

"Veretitsyn, such things are not done!"

"What things?"

"Did you ask for a leave?"

"I did."

"Why?"

"The provincial administration is boring, and my chest hurts."

"That is, the Khmelevskys left for the countryside."

"And I want to visit them. That doesn't concern you."

"But, isn't it true that you used my name to make the request of your supervisor?"

"Where did you hear that? I never even dreamed of doing that."

"You refer to my patronage. I know you, but I'm not going to pull strings for you. . . ."

quickly as possible. The dog began howling under the window every time she started to play.

Lolenka was glad that she had free time when she could go out to the garden and read. Mama had started to raise a ruckus over these little books, but Pelageya Semyonovna calmed her down. "So what if the young lady has an inclination? Let her at least in French. . . ."

Lolenka was indeed reading in French, the only thing she had—*Romeo and Juliet*. An idea had occurred to her, an idea that somehow made her feel ashamed: a book didn't have to be hidden when no one could understand what was in it and no one asked where it came from.

But what's so good about it? she had wondered during her first reading.

The words were complicated, always so tangled. Lolenka had studied everything diligently, especially French, because luckily there had been a satisfactory teacher. The teacher had given them many difficult passages and translations in class from their reader, from Chateaubriand;[3] but Lolenka still lacked the skill to understand everything without a dictionary. Still, she wanted to understand—she kept guessing; the further she went, the easier it became. . . . The content was charming, no doubt about it! However, when she read it the first time, it sparked her interest but didn't engage her. That first time cost her too much effort. She didn't cry over the love scenes or the final scenes. After finishing it, she didn't ponder over it, but details and words arose from her memory unexpectedly in fragments. Those details troubled her and made her smile. . . . Queen Mab—how charming! Wasn't she here somewhere in the grass on a chariot made from a shell and dragonfly wings? . . . Night, a dark vault, dawn, a lark—one after another seemed to flash before her eyes. . . .

"A rose is a rose, call it what you may,"[4] Lolenka recited, although she hadn't learned it by heart. "Throw away thy name, and for it, take all myself. . . .'⁵ My only hate became my only love. . . .''⁶

She snatched the book almost involuntarily and started to search for these words. She reread them, turned pages, read again.

"In the air of fate misfortune hangs over me. . . .''⁷

She threw the book onto the grass, lay facedown upon it, and started to cry bitterly, not for Juliet or Romeo, or herself; although she had felt heavy-hearted before, this was now completely forgotten. She was crying because, well, God only knew what in the world was going on, and this was so good, and God only knew why it was good. . . .

"The sunrise drives you out, and the sunset drives you back in," Mama said, catching Lolenka the next day when, even before matins, she had jumped up and was running out to the garden.

Lolenka didn't even try to see her neighbor; she didn't have time for him that day. But her neighbor didn't come that day or the following two days. This disconcerted Lolenka and strangely worried her, as though this had never happened before. But she felt that she absolutely had to find out what was wrong with him. How could she find out? From whom? There wasn't a single soul she could talk to in her neighbor's house, or anywhere. Up to this time Lolenka had needed no one's friendship. Maybe she didn't need it even now, but just to find out. . . . She needed to see him not to tell him something, but to ask what she should do, because living this way was impossible; everything around her was so terribly wrong. It had been the same before, true, but now, God only knew why, it was all somehow closer to her heart. Other people lived differently—that is, other people, not those like, well, Pelageya Semyonovna and her sons, the daughters of the archpriest, Olenka Belyaeva. The peasants seemed to live better. Lolenka had asked her new maid; she'd come to them straight from the countryside, and she said it was better there; they did what was important and useful there. . . . Well, why embroider this collar? Mama had no place to wear it; staying at home, she did her hair only once a week—the collar would waste away in her chest of drawers. You couldn't sell it—no one would buy it. If it was bought, what would the money be used for? Always food, firewood, candles. . . . Working for these things was necessary, of course, but why always talk only about that? Was there nothing else?

There really is nothing else for them to talk about, concluded Lolenka, and her heart felt as if it had been wrenched inside her.

She was alone; it was quiet; the clock was ticking—you could almost fall asleep. Suddenly a cry arose in the yard. Mama was angry with the children. Wailing resounded: the children were being beaten. . . .

"Good heavens! And it's the same thing every day!" Lolenka uttered loudly.

She jumped up from her embroidery frame, ran to her mother, and, completely in tears, intervened on her brothers' behalf. Mama was more than furious and ordered Lolenka back to the room.

"You see what a smart girl I've got!" exclaimed Mama. "Have your own children, then show off your intelligence! Try getting married, see how you like that!"

Will I really have children someday? Will I really live like this? Lolenka asked herself, looking with clouded eyes at her design after Mama's strong hand had forced her head down over the embroidery frame.

Papa returned home calmer than usual.

"Farforov got his permanent position," he said to Mama as he sat down at the table.

"Praise the Lord!" exclaimed Mama with delight. "So, what will Pelageya Semyonovna say now. . . ."

"Whatever she says, don't babble about it in front of this little goat." Papa pointed at Lolenka. "But now, I have to write to my sister. Where am I supposed to send it? Where's her letter?"

"Oh, good gracious! Where, really?" exclaimed Mama. "Alyona, where's Aunt Alyona Gavrilovna's letter? Good gracious! Where'd it get to! It was behind the mirror with our most sacred things. Those little brats probably ran off with it and tore it to pieces—now this is a real fix! How are we going to write to her now?"

The children swore they hadn't taken and torn up any letter. The search began. Mama was in despair; she rushed around, cursed her life, suspected that the letter had been stolen by someone for some reason. The crossbeams in the attic shook with Papa's voice. Papa ate and went to take a nap, after declaring that the letter would be found. Noise could be made, although Papa was sleeping: no noise could disturb him. Mama, therefore, did not restrain herself.

"You see, all this commotion is because of you, you unfeeling, foolish girl!" she said to Lolenka.

Lolenka felt completely perplexed, to the point of tears, and didn't understand why all this commotion was because of her, probably because Aunt Alyona Gavrilovna was her godmother. . . .

Mama dashed around, looking for the letter in the closets; the maid's trunk had already been searched. Left alone, Lolenka found the letter. It had simply slipped down behind the mirror where it had been shoved and fallen behind the chest of drawers that stood underneath. Lolenka was glad to have a moment of silence and didn't hurry to summon Mama and announce the find. She opened the letter to make sure that this was really it and, in passing, to find out what was so important in it besides her aunt's Petersburg address. There was nothing, really; best wishes for a happy Easter, news of her health, two words to the effect that there was nothing more to write about, and her address. Lolenka read it twice. . . . What nice handwriting my aunt has, every dot in its place! she thought while her ears hummed and her head spun.

Papa accepted the letter without any special sign of gladness and shoved it behind the mirror again. Although tomorrow was a mail day, Papa changed his mind and postponed the reply for when he had more time. He told Mama not to pester him and left to pay a visit, to have a cup of tea. Mama was angry at Papa for some time, because he didn't care about anything, and ran off to see Pelageya Semyonovna. Lolenka went out to the garden.

A fit of merriment came over her; suddenly all the unpleasantness was somehow forgotten. She felt like running, twirling around and around; if she'd been with someone, she would've laughed at any nonsense. She ran up to the fence and waited for her neighbor for a whole hour. He didn't come; his window was fastened securely.

What's happened to him? thought Lolenka. Has he gone visiting? Driven away somewhere? Some gentleman came to visit him once . . . perhaps he went to see him. It's easy to say; I haven't seen him for six days!

The gate creaked. Mama had returned.

Perhaps he came when I wasn't there, concluded Lolenka, running home.

She was being called. Mama had brought a bundle of cloth from Pelageya Semyonovna's house and was starting to cut out men's shirts. She gave one of these to Lolenka that night, ordering her to get up early and sew so Papa wouldn't see her. Lolenka thought this was made-to-order work and Mama wanted to hide from Papa the fact that she was working for money.

But why not work for money? Lolenka asked herself. Other people live that way. So what if Papa's a clerk?

But in place of these considerations, another came to mind. She could get up at daybreak and take the sewing out to the garden. She did just that. Mama saw this and told her that she was a smart girl. Lolenka didn't suspect that she was sewing a dowry for the suitor and that Mama was hiding it, fearing Papa's anger because the cloth had been bought on credit, because she had started doing things when no decision had yet been made, because she had not asked Papa's permission—many reasons. But the work went badly. Of course, Lolenka was always listening, not for Papa's footsteps—he never visited his garden—but for the least rustle on her neighbor's path. It was a glorious June morning. The bells had stopped ringing for the middle service at the monastery, meaning it was already eight o'clock. There was still a little time left and then it would be too late: at half-past eight the government workers left for their jobs. Her neighbor would also be leaving. . . .

His steps sounded behind the fence. Lolenka jumped up; the fabric flew onto the grass; a thimble and scissors went God knows where; the girl's hands got caught on the fence post. One of them was scraped so badly that it bled, but she didn't feel it.

"Ah! Lolenka!" said Veretitsyn when her little blushing face appeared from behind the fence.

"I thought you'd left," she said.

"Where? I'm not going anywhere."

"Why haven't you come? Six days. . . . Were you home all this time?"

"Yes, I'm not feeling well."

"Are you ill?"

From the first moment she'd noticed that he was pale and decided it meant nothing; at that moment she was thinking about nothing at all.

"What's wrong with you? . . . What illness do you have?"

"Nothing, really. But how are you?"

"All right. . . . But aren't you going to come out at all? That's terrible!" She felt like crying. "The weather, look how magnificent."

"What can I do? Good-bye, Lolenka!"

"Where are you going?"

"To the house. I'm going to lie down."

She followed him with her eyes, through the garden and into the yard. She saw him for one more moment when he opened the window in his room. He didn't appear again.

He's probably gone to lie down, Lolenka said to herself.

She sat down under the linden tree and sobbed bitterly. Let Mama or Papa come this very minute—she didn't care. Let them do whatever they wanted—she didn't care. She thought awhile about whether she should make some promise to God and, without thinking, made a large number of most unrealistic ones. Something, it seemed to her, had ended, and all of life had ended with it, because up to this time it had been possible to endure everything, both boredom and abuse, and she had needed no one. There had been something else, not just nonsense, gossip, and senseless studying. . . . And now he would die—and it would all be over.

Lolenka cried for so long that she forgot the time. She was being called to dinner. Mama waited on Papa to keep him in a peaceful mood, and that was why she didn't notice Lolenka's tearstained eyes. As soon as Papa had gone to lie down, Lolenka went out to the garden again. She remembered her work, found the scissors and thimble, and started to sew. The thought entered her mind that perhaps her neighbor would come again, that evening.

Evening came and went, but Veretitsyn didn't appear. Lolenka had long since abandoned her work and was looking at the light in his window.

"What are you doing here, counting the crows?" her mother exclaimed, appearing suddenly behind her.

Little work had been done; the "young lady" had been caught red-handed at someone else's fence. . . . She was punished for everything. Finally, since the secret was still being kept from Papa, she was ordered to sew, not in the garden, but in the servants' quarters, under the maid's supervision.

Three more days passed. On Sunday Lolenka was taken to the parish church service. A lady wearing the most beautiful red velvet cloak and straw hat with blond lace[1] and blue feathers attracted the attention of everyone in the church: such elegant attire was a rarity for a remote parish. The lady arrived late and behaved fashionably; she pushed a girl aside by the shoulders. Highly surprised by this act, the girl, wrapped in a woven shawl, then didn't know how to avoid the lady's swaying skirts. The lady leaned against the railing of the choir stall; she was getting tired of kneeling. She was brought two pieces of communion bread, and at the end of the service the church warden gave her a third piece with a deep bow.

"That's the treasurer's wife," Mama said to Pelageya Semyonovna. "Why isn't she in the cathedral?"

Mama was so interested in the appearance of such an important person that she barely responded to a bow from the young clerk Farforov. The clerk made an even deeper bow to the honorable treasurer's wife, but this elicited no response at all. He walked up to Lolenka, but she was looking at the treasurer's wife, too.

At this point the treasurer's wife honored a lady acquaintance with a reply: the lady was also dressed in velvet and was also asking why it had occurred to her to come here and why she wasn't in the cathedral.

"I was late," she said, trying to preserve an aristocratic immobility by barely opening her mouth and nodding her head only slightly to give a stately sway to her feathers. "I awoke late. I went to bed very late last night; I've been worried since the evening."

"Why?" asked her acquaintance.

"My brother is ill," the treasurer's wife answered reluctantly. "It's unpleasant enough that he's here, but now he's become much more sickly. . . ."

"What a cross for you to bear," another lady remarked with concern. Although unacquainted with the treasurer's wife, she couldn't resist the temptation of joining her little circle.

The treasurer's wife barely glanced at her and walked on.

Lolenka had grown deathly pale. The clerk Farforov attributed her silence to the pleasure afforded by his presence and explained to Mama: "She really does have a cross to bear. I work in the same department as her dear brother. He came here, you know, with the worst reputation . . . sent here because of his poetry . . . an extremely harmful person."

"I never hear anything over there at their house," remarked Mama. "He's probably quiet."

"My dear, he'd better be quiet!" Pelageya Semyonovna interjected. "He's living off his sister and brother-in-law."

"We thought," continued Farforov, "that he wasn't going to work because he was angry that they'd refused his request for a leave, but apparently he really is ill."

"It would probably be better if God took him!" added Pelageya Semyonovna.

"That would free them!" Mama concluded.

Lolenka stared at them. Mama talked about this again at home with the maid, then with Papa. Lolenka didn't eat anything the whole day, didn't say a word. Papa remarked to her: "What are you doing, little wolf cub, slinking about in the corners?"

For a whole week after that, Lolenka remembered nothing of what was happening around her, what was said to her, what was done with her. She didn't even know what she was doing; through force of habit, as soon as she had a free moment, she ran to the garden, to the fence. She returned to her work scarcely breathing and sewed silently until the next free moment. On those evenings when Papa and Mama left the house or Pelageya Semyonovna came to visit, Lolenka spent all her time at the fence. The window was barely lit; probably a night-light was burning.

On Sunday Mama didn't get ready for church; Lolenka was sent with Pelageya Semyonovna. Lolenka suffered from such impatience that she couldn't stand it any longer. She managed to escape Mama's watchful eyes, flew to the garden, and looked—Veretitsyn was sitting at his open window. . . .

"Well now, dear," Pelageya Semyonovna said that evening to Mama, "his mother was at church today. She marveled at your daughter: 'There,' she says, 'is a real zealot. If she bends her head any lower, she'll flip over. She went into the chapel, right up to the miracle-working icon. She bowed again and again to the ground; it was such a pleasure to watch.' I even said to the old woman, 'Look,' I said, 'what a treasure God is sending your son.' As bad-tempered as the old woman is, even she was surprised."

The next day Papa was particularly angry, because the letter to his sister, Alyona Gavrilovna, hadn't been written yet, although he was the one who was supposed to write to her; and finally he even did it. What was in his letter, no one knew. He even chased Mama away when she encroached upon his "peace and quiet" while he was busy with this matter. When he was finished, he called Lolenka.

"You, little French girl, very likely can't compose even two lines. Have you ever written to your godmother—well? No? Sit down, start writing here. You have to hold the pen properly. Write!"

Papa dictated and always used extremely long words; there was both "reverence" and "good intentions." It seemed to Lolenka that she was copying from Koshansky's rhetoric; she was enjoying herself for some reason, although it occurred to her for a second that her aunt might take her for a half-wit. When she signed herself "Your humble godchild and niece," Papa added two curly flourishes to these words in his own hand.

"Good gracious, this won't do!" exclaimed Mama after hearing the dictation. "There's nothing about a bestowal here at all."

"I wrote it! I wrote it, do you hear? I, the father, wrote it myself!" exclaimed Papa. "It's none of your business!"

He was so angry and upset that he ruined the address on two envelopes and ordered Lolenka to address a third, watching to see that this was done accurately, without mistakes. Lolenka worked hard; Vasilevsky Island,² the street name, and the intersection were shouted in her ears five times. Papa himself took the letter to the post office.

Lolenka soon forgot all this; she didn't hear Mama's sobs, that God only knew what was tangled up there in that letter, that nothing was said plainly, that Alyona would be left with nothing, that her aunt would "get away" perhaps with an icon or a hat, a hat that her aunt had perhaps previously worn but would only have restored a bit. Lolenka was sewing diligently and thinking, smiling. . . . Finally, when the sun's ascent signaled midday—the warmest, most salutary time—she stood up and said: "Mama, I'm off to the garden to work."

Pelageya Semyonovna was climbing onto the front steps, and she was not alone, but with a saleswoman and a large bundle. She and Mama had been examining and bargaining for a fur coat covered with a satin *doublé*³ for the last few days. Mama just waved her hand at Lolenka.

Lolenka had spent a few days at work in the garden; she'd found a little spot from which even the midday sun couldn't drive her. From this spot she had only to raise her head to see Veretitsyn's window directly. She began to notice what time it opened and closed; once she saw him eating dinner. Why she felt like crying as she watched this, why she then grew suddenly annoyed at herself for such foolishness, then amused and ashamed, again to the point of tears—God only knew. She finally became frightened; if Veretitsyn had come to the fence then, she would have run away.

One morning, pots of flowers appeared in the window. Lolenka managed to discern glory bower and heliotrope.

Probably his favorites, she thought. If only I'd known. . . . The heliotropes have been blooming at Olenka Belyaeva's for a long time. I could've gotten at least a sprig for him sometime when he came here. . . .

But the flowers covered the entire window. Only rarely a thin hand with a cup of water reached out and watered their roots carefully. Lolenka would have pulled them out by the roots.

Once, after dinner, at a time when everyone in her house was napping, when, as far as she could tell, even her neighbor was usually sleeping, Lolenka remembered his book, *Romeo and Juliet*, and ran back to get it. She didn't want to read from the beginning, and some parts in the middle didn't quite interest her, but she'd suddenly remembered scenes that, it seemed, had to be reread. She searched for them impatiently, started to read hurriedly, and it seemed strange to her that the language and style that had been so difficult before could now be understood without any trouble. Somehow they had been translated in her mind, in her heart, not into words, but into a sensation clearer and fuller than words. When Lolenka raised her head from the book, the branches of the linden tree darkening overhead frightened her. She didn't dare look at the window and suddenly ran out of the garden.

She didn't return until the next evening and then went only with the children, much farther away, and didn't approach the fence.

Mama had been saying for several days now that they had to dry linden blossoms⁴ for the winter, and she finally decided to go out to gather them.

"Take a shawl to collect them and a chair; you'll climb up, break them off," she said to Lolenka.

Mama plucked at the lower branches while Lolenka, standing on a chair, tried at least not to destroy the upper branches. Behind her in the neighboring garden the gate banged.

"You see, the brother of the treasurer's wife hasn't died," said Mama. "Smarty, don't fall on my head!"

Lolenka clung to the branches. Glancing around, she could see only that Veretitsyn was leaving the garden. He'd probably been there for a long time and could now take walks again. Therefore he might come tomorrow, but not early in the morning or late in the evening.

She could hardly wait for tomorrow. Veretitsyn walked around his garden twice; she was within two feet of him. She wanted to call out, to start speaking, and both times she hid behind the fence when he passed nearby. She was afraid. . . . The same thing was repeated on the following days. Veretitsyn came and lay down in the shade while Lolenka sat by herself in the shade and sewed. An hour, two hours, passed this way. Lolenka saw his gray coat, heard the rustle of his books. She wanted to call out but never could. She was afraid. . . . She stopped sleeping and began to cry at night.

Because of the coincidence of two holidays in a row, Papa went out of town. Mama got ready to make a pilgrimage on foot to a nearby monastery; her companion would be Pelageya Semyonovna; they would return in the evening. Lolenka asked to go with them; the many promises she'd made weighed heavily upon her, but the main thing was that she herself didn't know why she wanted to go away somewhere. She'd been feeling so unhappy that even the prospect of an entirely free day didn't gladden her. It wasn't that everything would really be so bad; she would have even felt miserable to the point of tears, leaving for the whole day, worrying about how things would be here without her, but she wanted to find out whether somehow all these tears and worries would make her feel better. . . . Mama refused to take her on very sensible grounds— who would look after the children?—and left at matins.

Lolenka had promised herself not to look after the children, but without even asking her, the children ran off to the neighbors' yards, and also without asking her, the maid took the three youngest off to the meadow. No dinner was prepared; cold leftovers from yesterday were enough for the children. Lolenka locked all the windows, the outside doors, the gate, took her sewing, and went out to the garden.

If someone knocks at the gate, I'll hear, she said to herself, and listened.

No one knocked at the gate to her yard. Her neighbor's footsteps sounded on the path, but not for long; he walked away into the shadows, lay down, and read. Lolenka calculated that she hadn't spoken with him for almost three weeks.

All the better, I'll get out of the habit, she thought. Why get used to foolishness? Really, it's impossible to live this way, thinking only about how to hang on to the fence, saying God knows what. I'm plainly not really learning anything, not housekeeping or any skills, and I'm almost sixteen years old. Decent people come along; we meet, but I don't know how to utter a word. I studied, but I've started to forget everything. I have to confess it all to Mama and Papa. Somehow, everything inside me has turned completely upside down. Do people really live this way at my age? Now, other young ladies . . .

Suddenly she brushed her work off her lap, crumpled it into a ball, threw it to the ground, and began to cry bitterly, almost wailing.

What kind of life is this? What's housework—swearing, nonsense, racket all day! What kind of people are these—Pelageya Semyonovna, this Farforov, a fool? What are studies but senseless memorization? Papa, Mama. . . . Good heavens, who would've said a word if it hadn't been for him, if it hadn't been for him. . . .

Lolenka ran to the fence. She hadn't managed to look over it when a voice sounded in her neighbor's garden:

"Aleksander Ivanych, where are you?"

Veretitsyn jumped out from behind the bushes very agilely for a man who'd not long ago been dying and rushed to meet the woman who was entering. She was young and wore a white dress with little blue and pink flowers; Lolenka discerned everything somehow all at once. The dress, simple and fluffy, flowed especially beautifully; the straw hat was also very simple, but round and broad—such things were never seen at that time in N. The guest seemed to light up the garden; because of her, everything all around seemed better.

"Sofya Aleksandrovna, what are you doing here alone?" asked Veretitsyn.

"I came from the country, alone," she answered.

Lolenka had never heard anything sweeter in her life than this voice: sonorous, tender, affectionate, something like the song of a bird, something like the voice of a child.

"I came to town to buy various things for work and, of all my friends, to visit only you, to find out how you are. Your sister, they say, isn't at home. You were in the garden; I asked to be taken to the garden. Well, so? How are you?"

"All right, I'm well now."

"You frightened us so. . . . We waited for you. . . . Just a second, here's a country gift for you."

She carefully unwrapped the large bundle of paper she was holding and drew out two large fresh roses.

"The first ones. I was so careful all the way here; I was afraid of crushing them."

Veretitsyn crushed them kissing her hands. From underneath the rim of her hat, her mouth and cheeks appeared fresher and more exquisite than the flowers.

"It's hot!" she said, taking off her hat. "Let's sit down somewhere."

Her hair was streaked rose gold in the sun; there was the same golden streak in her dark brown, nearly black eyes when she raised them, looking around.

Veretitsyn also looked around, but with annoyance at his bench.

"The sun," he said. "Where can we sit?"

"Here," she said, sitting down in the grass not far from the fence. "Will it stay shady here for half an hour?"

"And more. I can offer you a few comforts on my . . . well, really, not even my property."

"Listen, when are you coming to visit? Mama told me to be sure to invite you."

"Never, I think."

"Why not?"

"They won't let me!" answered Veretitsyn.

"How can that be? Last week. . . . Last week was Mama's name day. Some people were over at our house from town, including Ibrayev. I didn't know you were acquainted with him. Are you friends?"

"God had mercy on me," answered Veretitsyn.

"He asked about you and was sorry you weren't there. I said you were ill. He didn't know that. He was sure they'd given you a leave; he asked about it himself."

"That is, he lied to you so he might display the sensitivity of his heart and the freedom of his opinions at the same time. But, when it's inconvenient to flaunt it, he sings another tune. This friend and liberal said such frightful things about me to my superiors that they, relying on the word of such a man, decided that allowing me to leave the city for two weeks would be equivalent to unchaining a rabid dog. . . . I don't let him cross my threshold, this friend. He probably made sure he didn't speak about me before witnesses!"

Sofya didn't answer.

"You'll have to excuse me," Veretitsyn continued after a minute, "I have the foolish habit of telling you everything that's on my mind; perhaps I spoke out inappropriately just now."

"What do you mean?"

"Well, about Ibrayev. Perhaps I should've remained silent."

"Why?"

"It's just. . . . Perhaps you see him differently; he's a respectable man, from high society. . . . I've grown so uncivilized, stupid. I judge people according to their personal relationships with me: it's so narrow-minded, pitiful, petty. . . . Please, forgive me. I'll take it back if I said something offensive."

"Take back the last thing you just said," Sofya rejoined softly. "You're forgiven only because you were ill not so long ago and you're always irritated."

"That's just what I think, too; I'm irritated!" interrupted Veretitsyn. "Why is that? Really, what's there to be irritated about? After all, I'm really not an unrecognized great man. In 1852 A.D.[5] there's no such harvest of great men that greatness might even fall to my lot. My position, of course, is not very pleasant, but I don't deserve such honors of unhappiness: so, do I suffer much for very little? Do you know my history, then, Sofya Aleksandrovna?"

"Let's suppose that I do," she said, "but—"

"Allow me! Then, if I'm not unrecognized greatness, I'm nothing more than sensational mediocrity. Therefore, people like the honorable Ibrayev and company are perfectly right in refusing to associate with me, renouncing me: I'm not even interesting. To them, I'm a fool; I got caught in some nonsense like a petty thief. They've chosen a path for themselves and march along it valiantly, from their point of view. I acted valiantly, as it seemed to me, from my point of view; I drove Ibrayev away, but whether I was really right—"

"You're guilty toward yourself," interrupted Sofya.

"That's news. Please be so kind as to explain."

"I've already nearly said. . . . You're irritated at trivial things."

"But I've said the same thing," Veretitsyn rejoined, becoming incensed and starting to laugh. "I'm a petty person, so at the same time I'm venting my fury at others, I'm irritated at trivial things."

"Don't get angry, for goodness' sake," she interrupted meekly. "Tell the truth, confess: you're proud; you know your own dignity; how can you permit yourself—forgive me!—to lower yourself to the point of maliciousness toward some Ibrayev, a man whom you despise? Why corrupt yourself? Is he worth worrying about? Enough! It's painful to look at you: each and every trivial thing taken to heart! Start taking life easier."

"Let life be easier!" interrupted Veretitsyn. "You're reduced to triviality against your will. Really, it's not only Ibrayev—forgive me, Sofya Aleksandrovna . . . for telling you what I'm enduring because of trivial things . . . but then, spare me, it shouldn't be said aloud! Look, you're my guest, and you're sitting on the ground. If it wasn't for your books, I'd have forgotten how to read. . . . If I were one of those men who writes the laws . . . that kind don't grow petty on prison hulks,[6] at forced labor, but I—for me, even this has been enough! If it ever ends, I know I'll come out of it not as a man, but as an idiot, an animal."

"Stop!" rejoined Sofya. "This is despair. . . ."

"Despair is a deadly sin," he continued, starting to laugh. "Well, you're so good, pray for me sometime. 'Mention my sins in your prayers. . . .'[7] I know I'm ridiculous. This is my fate: foolish unhappiness, petty complaints, escape from everything—baseness. I'm preparing myself this way. Wait and see, I'll stand on my own two feet; they'll make me assistant head clerk for my reliable conduct, capabilities, and so forth and so on throughout this career. A frightened man, I'll learn to bow still lower; I'll have discovered the value of every cent, so I'll learn to steal, and everything will go just fine! Books corrupted me; well then, cast them aside! A game of preference[8] with my associates from work, recreation at a tavern on holidays—"

"Aleksander Ivanych, come to your senses," interrupted Sofya. "Is this really you?"

"It's me in the future," he answered, laughing, then turned away, examining a tall tuft of grass he was sitting beside.

"For goodness' sake!" she said after a minute, affection coupled with confusion causing her voice to tremble. "This is bad! Why are you tormenting yourself so uselessly? It only adds to all the grief!"

Veretitsyn didn't look around.

"Listen," continued Sofya, lightly touching his sleeve with her slender fingers, "God knows what you're saying about yourself. It's not true, and you know it isn't, so why say it? Does it really make you feel better? Can't you see that such talk only makes you feel worse?"

"It doesn't matter," Veretitsyn uttered softly.

"No, it does matter," she rejoined.

He turned around, grasped her hand fiercely, and began kissing it. Sofya kissed his head; tears welled in her eyes.

"Really, I'm not lecturing you," she said softly, "but what good is this? You must somehow be patient, wait."

"Wait for what?" he asked, still not raising his face from her hands. "For you to love me?"

She didn't gasp, didn't move, only glanced at him in fright. Their glances met.

"I love you. I've loved you for two years," Veretitsyn said firmly, "but will you never love me? Ever?"

Sofya was silent. He looked into her eyes.

"At least then there'd be something worth all the patience, something worth all the wait . . . but then, you'll never love me, will you?"

She remained silent. He was pale as death; he was choking but continued firmly, looking at her the whole time.

"I would try to remain a decent man, not becoming boorish or dull; I would preserve my strength to be in a condition to earn an honest crust of bread: I know you would be satisfied with such a crust. . . . I wouldn't have to wear myself out physically because it's already come to that."

"I will love you," she uttered, having also grown pale.

"From compassion? From selflessness?" he exclaimed with his strange laugh. "I humbly thank you, that's not necessary!"

"Why do you think—"

"But then you don't know how to lie," interrupted Veretitsyn. "I've been looking you in the eyes for a whole hour! Enough, don't force yourself: it's unnecessary; I'm afraid of selflessness. I'm a bad man—I wouldn't know how to pay for it. I don't know how to be grateful! Please don't imagine that your goodness obliges you to make sacrifices: I've already understood this to be a sacrifice. I'm not asking for it. I know you're perfect. . . . Perfection makes us sinners very miserable!"

She stood up. "Listen—"

"Why listen!" Veretitsyn exclaimed. "I know you! Why do I love you if it isn't for this goodness, this perfection, this truth? Well, tell the truth outright: you don't love me, do you?"

"No," she answered, bowing her head, with tears in her eyes.

"Well, then, that's fine! I won't uselessly attempt to obtain it any longer: love can't be forced. What's not, just isn't. . . . Forgive everything I've said, and good-bye—apparently you want to leave now?"

Sofya suddenly turned around and held out her hands to him.

"If you only knew," she said in tears, "I can't . . . it's so painful."

"Don't force yourself; after all, it's not your fault!" answered Veretitsyn, and began to laugh.

"You're cruel!" she said, sobbing.

"That makes it all the more forgivable to leave me to the mercy of fate," he rejoined.

"Listen, come visit us, drive out to see us! I'll do everything in my power, everything to console you as before. . . ."

"Why should I tease myself, Sofya Aleksandrovna? The only thing that can comfort me is not in your power. Don't worry about me."

"But what will happen?"

"Do you think I'll be unhappy? Never mind. This vegetable garden will be here, this house, the provincial administration. . . . Perhaps not for very long!"

"I love you!" she exclaimed.

"Don't lie," he rejoined.

She pressed her face into her hands and ran to the gate. Veretitsyn didn't move from the spot. "If you'd been telling the truth," he said after her, laughing and loudly, "you wouldn't have left!"

Lolenka, who had been sitting on the ground, stood up, holding on to the fence. Her legs felt weak at the knees; her heart was pounding; her head was throbbing; she felt cold.

"I feel delirious," she said to herself.

Her lips, which had moved to utter this, suddenly pressed together convulsively. She cried out and ran back to the house.

She tossed and turned on her bed for two hours and sobbed, unable to calm down. The maid returned, knocked, and was obliged to climb over the fence to open the gate and admit the children, whom she assembled and led to dinner. Seeing the young lady's tears, the maid supposed that, left alone, the young lady had been frightened by something, and to keep from getting in trouble, she ordered the children not to tell Mama and Papa when they returned that their sister had been crying; they'd want to know why everyone had gone off and left the house. Her reason was sensible, and besides, for the children, their older sister's tears were of little importance. Lolenka stood up weak, as if ill. Toward evening she tidied up what was necessary so Mama wouldn't be angry when she returned. Then she went out to the garden, found her work, and sat with it by the window in her room. Mama returned with Pelageya Semyonovna; they had brought home a large amount of communion bread. Because of the occasion of Papa's absence, Pelageya Semyonovna stayed the night. They drank tea for a very long time, ate supper, and talked despite their fatigue. This fatigue made itself known by about ten o'clock with snoring that resounded throughout the entire house.

Lolenka lay down and got up again; everything was quiet, of course, only in their house and the lane. Noise still could be heard in the distance: revelers were returning home; the city had not yet quieted down. Soft moonlight shone through the slats in the shutter. Lolenka dressed in the dim light, threaded her way past the sleeping children, opened the door onto the front steps, and went out. The dog began to growl and, recognizing her, settled down again.

"I'll go away somewhere," said Lolenka.

She looked around at the narrow deserted yard, at the locked gate. The moon shone pale, as it always did on summer nights; nothing stirred in the air; the noise died down in the distance gradually; Lolenka became frightened: never in her life had she been alone like this, without permission, at night.

"I'll go away somewhere," she repeated, trembling and as if asking herself whether she could summon the daring for this, "but, where?"

She covered her face with her hands and suddenly recalled that the beautiful woman she'd seen this morning had made the exact same gesture, had left with the exact same tears. . . . What does she have to cry about! Let her try putting up with . . .

Lolenka felt like racing about, sobbing, crying out; not knowing what she was doing, she found herself running out to the garden, the familiar path. The strangest thoughts spun around in her head, one after another. She wanted to die; she wanted someone to die, so that, well, everything would end, right there and then, because it was impossible to live like this. . . . She was running. God only knew why these words suddenly occurred to her, but she still liked them so much: "Love flies toward the object of love like a school-boy runs from a book. . . ."[1]

Detestable book where this was written! This book, crumpled, folded in four (as she'd been instructed!), was here in her pocket. It was accustomed to lying there. . . . Lolenka snatched it out and, taking off at full speed, hurled it over the fence into the neighboring garden. It was as if she'd torn out her own heart and thrown it away. The pages of the book barely rustled, falling lightly onto the grass. Lolenka kept looking for one moment more to see where it landed and clutched the fence to keep from falling. Veretitsyn was walking along his path, his eyes downcast, and didn't turn his head at the rustling sound.

"He's always brooding over her!" Lolenka said, looking back at him as his figure, moving off into the distance, blended into the twilight. "Always over her. . . . Would it ever occur to him to ask whether it's been easy here? Who caused all this? If it hadn't been for him, if he'd never spoken and gotten me all confused. . . . That'll show him! It's good that God punished him. . . ."

Tears rolled down her face, one after another.

"Let him see what it's like having everything taken away! Everything is bad, life is bad—let him feel the same! He laughs at everything—there, let this woman laugh at him! At times . . . at times, my whole heart would leap whenever he said anything. . . . Why did he talk to me? Why would he drive such a poor abandoned girl to grief? Well, let him chat with his beautiful women! What business is it of his if I study Koshansky or not? Really. . . . Good Lord! Did it really make him any more cheerful to prove that I knew nothing? He ruined my character . . . but he should've understood that each one of his words was like a knife in my heart, that after him I really couldn't look at anyone else. . . . Apparently, he's an intelligent man; he should've understood. So, he had to. . . . Well then, let God punish him, let something even worse happen to him. . . ."

She sobbed, and suddenly noticing that her neighbor had stopped and seemed to be listening, she ran headlong from the garden to the house and cautiously made her way back to her bed. There, in the darkness of the warm room, she couldn't sleep; another concern had occurred to her: What had she done, throwing away the book like that? Well, if he didn't find it, the dogs would tear it up, and he'd send for it sometime or ask for it himself. . . . No, he wouldn't ask for it; he wouldn't show his face in the garden. Well, he'd send for it; Papa would ask from whom. . . .

The problem began to assume a fantastic character; fatigue and the late hour did their work. Lolenka fell asleep.

The next day was that other holiday that obliged the family with Papa's absence. Papa's absence seemed to have a festive, calming influence, too. Pelageya Semyonovna stayed all day. It was the Fast of St. Peter,[2] but because of the occasion of Papa's absence and the holiday, Mama had gone to the market early in the morning to buy some fish. While Mama was busy in the kitchen, Pelageya Semyonovna expressed a desire to chat with the daughter, to test her in the domestic arts.

"So, my angel, do you know how to cook a meal like your mama?"

Lolenka could prepare a few things, and even better in theory; in practice, her mother never let her touch anything, and now Mama, overhearing the question, responded, "My dear! Let this little sophisticate do it and she'll fix something even the dog won't eat."

"That's right, a real lady!" Pelageya Semyonovna rejoined, smiling pleasantly. "Well, my angel, are you practicing your music? Why don't you play a little polka, I'll listen. The church service, it seems, is over: it's all right."

Lolenka started to play; the dog began to howl.

"What's she doing, your dog?" exclaimed Pelageya Semyonovna, and opened the window into the yard, entertained by the dog's frenzy. "You really have a fickle dog!"

Pelageya Semyonovna was delighted and listened to the dog throughout the entire polka.

"And do you read French, my angel? Well then, read, I'll listen. Even if I don't understand, I'm always flattered."

"Why should I if you don't understand it, Pelageya Semyonovna? . . ."

"I don't want to hear any of your arguing!" responded Mama.

"I don't even have a book. . . ."

"How can that be! Nonsense! What about the one you've been reading all the time? Read it now!"

Lolenka's throat tightened, her ears burned with fury and anguish. Right then, right then, she would've run away somewhere but didn't have the strength! She didn't want to cry but scream, tear out her hair . . .

"Don't upset your mother," Pelageya Semyonovna told her in a whisper. "Well, that's some character you've got! You'd better break that habit, my angel, break it—tone yourself down! You'll have to live with your husband and his family. . . . Don't get caught within reach of your husband—you'll gain nothing. It's easy to accept from your papa and mama, but from a husband . . . oh, that's really difficult! I know. . . . Read just three little lines, my beauty."

Lolenka started to read her French grammar book aloud; tears fell on the book thick and fast. Pelageya Semyonovna shook her head in the direction of the kitchen, amused by the foreign words.

"Look at her go, so smart!" she said. "Well, that'll be enough, my beauty; we've been entertained. Just submit, you have to submit," she added in a whisper. "But now you and I are off to the garden, the little garden green, we're off to walk away sadness and misery."

"I'm not going out to the garden," Lolenka rejoined.

Pelageya Semyonovna took her arm and led her outside. "What cherries you're going to have this year!" she said, dragging the girl after her. "You'll have to lock the gate to the garden, my child; at least you'll tie up your dog here when they start to ripen. That's some fence you've got; well, the treasurer's kids will climb over here in no time and pick them. And those roughnecks, they're worth about as much as your children! . . . Watch out for them. Look, that's some neighbor-cavalier you've got strolling around there. Really, it goes without saying, so good-looking! I suppose, you, my angel, have never seen him, the brother of the treasurer's wife! There he is—he seems to be watching, it seems, from a distance. He's nothing to look at. Do you need someone like that? You need someone strong and handsome, a good man, but that one. . . . Well, God forgive you! You just look and you sin; only yesterday I went to church to pray to God over 'deeds' just like this which they have pictured there. . . .³ It seems you have sugar peas planted here, my beauty, did I see beds? Yes, it seems so, and have they started to ripen? It's good to amuse yourself sometimes. . . ."

Pelageya Semyonovna made her way to the beds; Mama called her in to eat some *pirog* and ordered Alyona to pick and bring whatever peas had ripened.

Lolenka was left alone and stood hanging her head. It was quiet all around her, except for a bird singing, but then even the bird fell silent, and the footsteps on the neighboring path now could be heard all the more clearly. . . .

What have I done? Lolenka suddenly asked herself. I'm bored, but then he's bored, too. Why shouldn't I look at him?

She walked toward the fence, becoming quieter and more timid as she approached, but still she approached. Veretitsyn was approaching also. Lolenka became frightened: he had *Romeo and Juliet* in his hands, and it was already impossible to run away.

"Hello," said Veretitsyn in his usual joking tone. "Well now, did you throw this away by mistake instead of Koshansky?"

"It fell," uttered Lolenka, and somehow involuntarily reached for the book.

"Ten feet away and to the side?"

Veretitsyn smiled softly and shook his head.

Let him say, "Don't lie," like he did yesterday, to her . . . thought Lolenka at that second.

Veretitsyn probably remembered, too.

"Do you need it?" he asked her seriously and sharply.

"No," Lolenka answered, also sharply.

"Didn't you like it? Should I bring you the *Tale of Prince Bova?*"[4]

"You're always making fun of me. You've always been making fun, from the very first day. . . . I still don't know why," she said, suddenly distressed to the point of tears so that all her annoyance passed.

"I'm sorry," answered Veretitsyn, and turned to leave.

"No, listen, listen," she repeated, even reaching out her hand to stop him. "What have you done to me? . . . What have you driven me to? . . ."

"Did they catch you with this book and make you stand in the corner?" he asked.

"Good Lord! Would you hear me out seriously at least for one minute! . . . Thanks to you, I've begun to think, to understand such terrible things . . . about myself, my home, my father, my mother. . . . But then, I'm so unhappy! If you, you, at least . . . if from you I saw . . . but you—"

"Lolenka, I'm miserable enough without you, too; enough of all this fickleness," interrupted Veretitsyn.

"So thank God you're miserable," she exclaimed, beginning to sob.

"Well now, that's nice," he answered, "you'll get over it. Good-
bye."

He left the garden, slamming the gate. Lolenka was reminded of
the clatter of a hammer she'd heard once in her life at a funeral.
Why she was reminded of this, what was happening to her—she
didn't know. She wanted to leave but couldn't; she sat on the
ground, oblivious of everything. Her mother came to get her and,
finding her in tears, became frightened and took her back inside the
house.

"What's the matter with you? What's wrong, Alyona, Alyonush-
ka?"

Pelageya Semyonovna remarked to Mama in a whisper that
probably the young lady had found out about the suitor, had heard
about him somehow, and because of that—a girlish concern—was
grieving over it.

"That's true," said Mama. "Come here, my little fool . . . well
now, come here."

Lolenka came out from behind the partition where she had been
lying down.

"Have you heard about Viktor Martynych?"

"That's nothing to cry about, dear, since he's such a handsome
man," added the guest.

"And the finest man, with money. I daresay you'll be living like
a lady. You have God to thank for sending you such a mate. Who
do you think you are? It's shameful even to show you in public: this
is the mercy of God watching over you. What's there to howl
about? You've begun this too early; let Assumption Day[5] pass, Farforov will get his permanent position and you'll turn sixteen; well
now, you can carry on about it all day long, then. But whether you
carry on about it or not, I'm still marrying you off. There now, I'll
tell your father, try that if you keep on like this! Your father will be
in no mood for jokes; you still don't know him well enough."

"And your godmother will send some *bourre de soie*[6] from Petersburg for that special day; we'll make a wedding dress—oh! with flounces," the guest interjected.

"Mama, you can kill me right where I stand, but I won't marry Farforov!" uttered Lolenka very firmly. . . .

Eight years had passed since that time.

In the middle of last August, on one of those bright warm days that occur in Petersburg before the beginning of autumn, an unusually large crowd of visitors had gathered inside the halls of the Hermitage.[1] There were well-dressed ladies, amazing for the width of their hoop skirts, swaddled in circular-shaped mantillas; young ladies amazed at nothing, laced to immobility in their fashionable Cossack-style jackets and showing signs of life only by the rather inharmonious tapping of their heels on the marble and parquet; radiant and rather noisy youths, the companions of these ladies and young women; ladies less finely dressed but with a noticeable claim to the right to knowledge and understanding, with a loud enthusiasm for names; the young ladies with them, who were somewhat sad, and the children, who were somewhat frightened, and their companion, almost always explaining the art objects in the manner of an expert, with all the confidence of authority, at great length and not always intelligibly; provincial men and women with unfeigned emotion and old-fashioned attire; the common people—townsfolk, servants, craftsmen—going from painting to painting and from statue to statue, their entire company without fail composed indivisibly of five people, all quite satisfied with the room attendant's explanation; very respectable and serious people, in pairs, rarely in

threes, unhurried, who looked at one object for a long time, returned from distant rooms to something that had caught their attention and talked among themselves so softly, so animatedly and
apparently so knowledgeably, that the artists, who were situated
near the walls with their easels, stools, brushes, and paints and who
were diligently at work copying the great masters, were compelled
to look around involuntarily. The artists frequently had trouble
with the visitors: an easel in front of a painting evoked curiosity
from even the most indifferent visitors, particularly the ladies.
They all without fail wanted to see why there was an easel and perhaps even take a look. Courtesy required moving off to the side; if
they could manage without it, the artists had to listen to comments
and conversation over their heads, sometimes even humorous,
always finally tiresome. . . . But together, the wandering, comment-
ing visitors and the working artists enlivened those charming halls
on a bright day; the wonders of art looked condescendingly from
the dark red walls upon both the initiated and the uninitiated; beauty radiated equally for everyone in eternal images as something
higher, forgiving the profane word, the clever comment, as well as
the courage of the student copyist.

A young man wandered through the Spanish room. He was completely alone and, apparently, had met no acquaintances because he
hadn't spoken with anyone while walking around the entire Hermitage. . . . It was already getting late; there were fewer visitors all
the time; they went off either to the galleries with the precious gems
or downstairs to the statuary. Soon only the attendant by the door,
two or three artists at work, and the young man remained in the
Spanish room; in the silence, the footsteps of people passing
through the corridor, the light rustle of a falling brush, and the
scrape of a bone knife on a palette could be heard; the sun shone especially softly through the sailcloth on the glass ceiling and scattered sparks on the gold frames, revealed pale faces on the dark can-

vases. The young man leaned against a vase of lapis lazuli in the middle of the room, after selecting a spot to get a better view of Murillo's small *John with the Lamb*,[2] a painting always concealed by copyists' easels. Even now an easel stood opposite it, but to the pleasure of the viewer, there was no artist. The young man transferred his gaze from this painting to another almost next to it, also by Murillo: *The Young Christ and the Young John*,[3] reaching out to embrace each other. It was apparent that he was comparing and selecting his favorite of two favorite paintings. He seemed to make up his mind and moved a few steps to the left to see the second painting more closely; an easel stood opposite it, too, but fortunately didn't conceal it. The divine faces of the children with their goodness, tenderness, and kindness, the round, joyful little heads of angels in a cloud, the frisky lamb in the corner of the painting, now produced not delight, but something more—the feeling of a kind of conciliatory joy on the young man's face. He looked without noticing that he was being observed, almost as attentively. An artist sat behind the easel in front of the painting; she had already glanced over a few times at the young man as he walked by, stood at the vase; but now, when he paused almost behind her shoulders, forgetting himself in his contemplation of Murillo, she turned around completely and looked into his face.

"Monsieur Veretitsyn, if I'm not mistaken?" she said.

He took his eyes away from the painting.

"Madame. . . . Mademoiselle . . ."

"Lolenka," she finished, and offered her hand.

"It's you!" he nearly shouted.

"You haven't forgotten?"

"I remember, I remember well! But . . . it can't be. . . . What are you doing here?"

"As you see. Sit down while I put my palette away."

She pointed to a velvet divan under a painting.

"It is you!" repeated the astonished Veretitsyn. "But how did it happen? . . . You've hardly changed! . . . How many years has it been?"

"Eight. I've been living here with my aunt for eight years."

"In Petersburg? I've been living here for two years myself."

"What are you doing?"

"I work, teaching young people."

"That's wonderful. And I study."

"And look what success."

"Yes, of course, I couldn't have expected this from myself in N. How did you get away from there?"

"They finally let me go. I tried to obtain a position for about a year—finally I found one. But how did you get the idea of moving?"

"I believe," she rejoined, smiling, "that the air in N. is unhealthy and everyone should try to escape it. I at least promised myself that I'd never go back there again."

Her eyes shone and reminded Veretitsyn of the former Lolenka, her childish anger, their meetings over the fence. She really had grown very little; her face had hardly changed; rather, her dress and elegant hairstyle had changed her. But it seemed awkward to Veretitsyn to say directly what he was thinking after her last words, and he merely asked, "And your father and mother?"

"They're living, back there. Are you married, Aleksander Ivanych?"

"No. Are you, Elena? . . ."

"Vasilyevna. No. What are you doing today? Are you free?"

"Until this evening. I have a public lecture this evening."

"Oh, what an honor for you! Why didn't I know about it? Where is it?"

"At one of the schools on Vasilevsky Island."

"But I live on Vasilevsky Island; why didn't I know? So, has it been just recently?"

"I begin today."

"It's time for me to go home now. Let's go together; dine with us and then go to your lecture this evening. Would you like to?"

"I'd be delighted."

Lolenka fastened her box of paints securely, glanced over at Veretitsyn, and smiled.

"Have I changed a lot, Elena Vasilyevna?"

"You've aged. Let's go. . . . Oh, this is such a bother to carry!"

She called the attendant and handed him the bottles of oil to store away until tomorrow.

"You're used to everything here just as if you were at home," remarked Veretitsyn.

"I've been coming here every day for a whole year."

"Are you studying?"

"Yes, and I'm making copies on order. I'm working," she finished while Veretitsyn, in parting, glanced at Domenichino's *Cupid*[4] near the doors from the corridor to the Italian room.

"Hold this, I'm going to get my hat," Lolenka said, giving him the box when they had come down the staircase, and went into a side room.

Veretitsyn, standing in the entryway, looked at the magnificent white marble staircase with the colonnade above: through the open upper doorway the red wall of the Italian room and Andrea del Sarto's *Madonna*[5] could be seen. Sad, she looked straight ahead while the Christ child, almost standing on her lap, turned away. Her glance accompanied those leaving. . . .

"Do you like art?" Lolenka asked when she returned. "Why don't you come here more often?"

"I never have time."

"It's nice when there's so much to do!" she continued, dashing down the front steps. "What a lovely time of year! We'll reach the embankment sooner to the right."

Veretitsyn walked in silence. The more he looked at Lolenka, the more she amazed him. It wasn't the unexpectedness of the meeting or the sharp contrast with the past, which so clearly brought to mind in these minutes much that had been forgiven in the past: what amazed him was the change in this girl—adept, bold, self-assured.

Well, how they grow! he thought, bowing his head involuntarily.

Lolenka rested her arms on the granite and looked down at the water; Veretitsyn did the same.

"It was like this at the fence," he said.

"Yes, only we never stood side by side!" she rejoined, and burst out laughing. "How long ago, it's awful! What a chaotic time! Remember how often you were in such low spirits. That doesn't happen now, does it?"

"Why wouldn't it?"

"Now, when you have interests, work, when you're on your own, when you're useful, independent—I don't understand it!"

"What can I do! That's just the way it is."

"And why is that?"

"I'm thirty-four, not twenty-four, Elena Vasilyevna."

"That's no reason," she rejoined, shaking her head.

"No, it is a reason. An unexpected, undeserved unhappiness happened to appear during your youth and exhausted you for seven years. It's easy to say: take seven years away from somebody! The best years of life without any occupation, without books, God knows in what kind of society, without the right to think, let alone speak! You have to experience what it's like yourself to judge whether it would be easy, whether it's possible to recover. . . . You yourself said it was a chaotic time! I must be one of the hardy ones because I came away from it with only melancholy and bitterness."

She was shaking her head all the time and smiling.

"Even in a life correctly lived," Veretitsyn continued, "when looking back on youth from middle age, there's a great accumulated deficit in terms of the realization of various hopes and ideals, but even more in a life such as . . ."

He stopped.

"Are you laughing, Elena Vasilyevna?"

"I definitely don't understand this," she rejoined, raising the heavy box into her arms again. "Don't worry, I'll carry it: I don't like to be obliged to others for things I can do myself. . . ."

"The old rule says: 'Don't do anything yourself that you can make others do,'"⁶ Veretitsyn responded, laughing. "Give me the box."

"Oh, your old rules!" she interrupted, no longer joking and displaying special enthusiasm. "All our wrongs, all the misfortunes of our generation, occurred because of them! You supported those rules, you submitted to them, you carried things to the point that we had to fight and suffer in order to escape from under that oppression, and design for ourselves some possibility of living more easily! . . . You say it was hard for you then and it's hard for you now, that you're a broken people. Why did you allow yourselves to be broken? Why didn't you renounce your prejudices, conquer your weakness, work more energetically? You're bored, full of melancholy and bitterness because you're always regretting something and remembering something; you'd like to protect some old thing you've grown accustomed to! You were always miserable and dreaming and finally became so lazy that you couldn't work—"

"You were always singing; now that's an occupation!" interrupted Veretitsyn. "And the younger generation advises us to dance?'"

"The younger generation is not egotistical," she answered, becoming embarrassed and offended like the former Lolenka.

"But then the older generation wasn't always just miserable and dreaming," Veretitsyn rejoined. "Good for you, the new saplings; but don't scold the broken ones who are in pain in any weather. . . . We're philosophizing, Elena Vasilyevna."

"And have even slipped into poetry," she added.

"Oh, time! This never happened at the fence: apparently you enjoyed reading Kheraskov. . . ."[8]

"What nonsense! Impossible! . . . No, you know, I'm very glad I ran into you; I remember you, but I don't want to remember that time. It brings back so many absurdities. . . . It's past—and finished! I live in the present."

"By the way, in the present, tell me about your aunt. You're taking me to meet her."

"My aunt, a good and intelligent woman, was married to an intelligent, well-educated man. She came here with him and tried to educate herself for him. I give her a lot of credit for this. She came to N. to get me and took me to her home that summer when you and I were seeing each other. There's a good boarding school in the building where she lives; she sent me there to study. They noticed that I had an aptitude for painting; I started attending an art school—and, as you see, I paint at the Hermitage. I know three foreign languages; I translate and prepare compilations. I earn so much doing this that I can say I'm not an extra burden at home: my aunt isn't rich. Our society consists of the professors from the boarding school where I studied, their families, artists—all busy people. That's why free time is so dear to them and they try to spend it pleasantly. Once a week we get together at my place. Join us."

Veretitsyn thanked her with a bow.

"So, life is easy for you?" he asked.

"Of course! I'm free!" answered Lolenka. "I'm not obligated to anyone for anything. My aunt, it's true, gave me my education, but since she had the means, she should have done this, and I had the right to accept. But from the time I was able, I've worked for myself: I don't cost her a thing. I even earn enough for my entertainment: for example, I subscribed for a two-year season's ticket for a gallery seat at the opera; my aunt decided to surprise me this year and paid for me. I said nothing to her, but sold my copy of a Greuze[9] and obtained another two seats in the box of some friends, under the pretext that I wanted to listen to the opera twice. But she understood that she shouldn't embarrass me even with the intention of doing something nice. . . . Do you go to the opera?"

"Rarely. I never have time."

"If you plan your time well, you'll be able to get enough," continued Lolenka. "Here's our apartment. Will you remember the way?"

She went in and began to climb the steep staircase of one of the tallest buildings on Middle Prospect. Veretitsyn followed her. It would be impossible to forget this ascent, and the thought occurred to Veretitsyn that it would have been better for Lolenka to say, "If you would be so kind," thus requesting her guest's forbearance.

Lolenka rang the bell. A housemaid opened the door and took Veretitsyn's coat.

"Elena Gavrilovna isn't at home," she said.

"Has she been gone a long time?"

"Yes. She said she would have dinner at a friend's home and go to the theater in the evening and for you to come to the theater, if you'd like; she left a note there."

"I wouldn't like to," answered Lolenka. "Let's have dinner."

She invited Veretitsyn to come in. The drawing room was nicely furnished with a lot of greenery in the corners and windows; the table, already set, awaited Lolenka; the housemaid provided another place setting for Veretitsyn.

"Sit down; I'm very hungry," Lolenka said to him.

As she ate, she pulled a page from a newspaper off a nearby table and read aloud, in fragments; a very lively conversation about the Italian war and Italian freedom began. Lolenka knew and continually read a great deal. The dinner passed imperceptibly in this discussion. The sunny day turned autumnal toward evening: the patch of sky over the chimneys of the neighboring building paled and grew dark; the windows fogged up.

"Let's go to my room," said Lolenka, getting up from the table. "I'll order a fire lit; we've talked a lot about Italy, but even in the winter it doesn't get any colder there than this."

Her room was next to the drawing room—a living room, workshop, and study all together. There were a few framed paintings on the walls, unfinished sketches and canvases turned facedown on the floor, a portrait just begun on an easel—probably of her aunt; a palette was hanging coquettishly on the fretwork of a mirror; plaster busts, statuettes, molds of ancient heads had been placed on shelves and pedestals. A large desk and two bookcases in the corners were filled with books; a couch and a few cozy armchairs had been moved comfortably near the fireplace. Only that corner alone suggested relaxation; all the rest reiterated the idea of strenuous, uninterrupted work calculated by the clock. Lolenka actually glanced at the clock.

"I'll get you some tea," she said to Veretitsyn at the threshold and left, letting him go in if he wished.

Returning, she found him in the middle of the room; he was looking all around.

"Not bad, isn't that true?" she asked. "The landlord was kind enough, in accordance with my wishes, to hang red wallpaper in here—a pale likeness to the walls of the Hermitage! On Tuesdays I entertain company and light the room *a giorno*[10]—it looks magnificent. . . . Were you thinking how magnificent it looks?"

"Tell me, is this you?" interrupted Veretitsyn. "Really, at times I don't believe my eyes! This is a rebirth!"

"What's so special about it?" she replied with surprise.

"But just remember . . ."

"I remember nothing," she answered. "Haven't I said that already? If people have an inclination to remember, let them recall their character from childhood and then it will be clear that what happens to them is the only thing that could happen. . . . If you had known me, you wouldn't be surprised that I've cast off my yoke and choose not to remember anything about it."

"Yes, it's been painful for you, difficult—"

"You're thinking about my family?" she interrupted. "There's nothing painful or difficult! I don't remember, so I don't burden my memory, just as I don't remember all the nonsense I've heard or read. . . . Does this seem strange to you?"

"Not strange, but rather decided."

"Not at all! It's magnanimous."

Veretitsyn looked at her while she adjusted the coals in the fireplace; twilight and the fire cast a strange light in the red room; this light and the sharp shadows were becoming to the young woman's animated face. She sat down, curling up quietly in an armchair; a desire for rest, enjoyment of rest, but not contemplation, showed in her movements and gaze.

"Well, let's reminisce about the old days," she said after a silence and smiling. "What about Mademoiselle Sophie?"

"Sophie?" repeated Veretitsyn.

"Yes, Sophie, Sofya . . . Aleksandrovna . . . but the last name . . ."

"Khmelevskaya," said Veretitsyn. "How do you know her?"

"I saw her," Lolenka answered, laughing. "What's so unusual

about the fact that, living in N., I knew Sofya Khmelevskaya? . . . I saw her with you in your garden."

"Ah!" said Veretitsyn, looking at the fire.

"It seems that she was a remarkable girl, perfection itself?"

"Yes."

"Educated, talented, intelligent?" continued Lolenka. "Tell me, where is she now? In this day and age, when . . ."

"And so on and so forth," Veretitsyn prompted.

"Yes," Lolenka confirmed without smiling, "in this day and age a woman like that could do so much, act—a highly evolved woman with a clear gaze, with this truth which was amazing in her, with an unwomanly straightforwardness—not only by her example, any one of her words. . . . She's not here in Petersburg?"

"No, she's in the country. She's married."

"Married!" exclaimed Lolenka.

"Married," repeated Veretitsyn.

"Who's the fortunate man who's been so honored as to possess this perfection?"

"A nice fellow, a landowner in N."

Lolenka lifted herself up from her seat.

"Monsieur Veretitsyn! . . . And this is perfection? . . ."

"More than ever," he answered softly, without taking his eyes from the fire.

"That perfection is a woman who sold her will, plunged into a void . . ."

"She didn't sell it, but only gave it away: her mother pleaded with her, and she could give in: she loved no one. Her husband is an honest man, not stupid . . . well, not progressive, of course, not a public figure. . . . But then, why always give the treasure away to the rich: the poor need it more."

"What exactly has she done for those poor?"

"She gave her mother a peaceful corner until her death, reconciled her husband with his father, made the old man behave more like a human being, taught her husband to study, as much as was within his means, gave those who depended on them a breathing space—"

"Oh, great deeds!" interrupted Lolenka. "And to waste oneself on this? On tidying the bedroom for Mama, reconciling the family, curbing blows, teaching her husband the alphabet? All this, for a higher being. . . ."

"Who's to say all this isn't for a higher being?" Veretitsyn rejoined. "Those lower wouldn't know how to accomplish it or would find it distasteful! Those who sacrifice themselves till the end are higher; only sacrifices of perfection lead to something."

"These sacrifices have gone on for several thousand years!" said Lolenka.

"That's why it's easier now than it was a thousand years ago," answered Veretitsyn. "Little by little, but the impact, the memory, remains."

"A comforting 'little by little'!" rejoined Lolenka. "These are simply excuses, the great deeds of egotists, lazy people who don't want to take on more important matters! Just wait, you'll see, how, in a few years, Sophie, your perfection, reconciles herself, grows dull. . . ."

"She would sooner die!" exclaimed Veretitsyn.

"And what good would her death do? Her husband will marry someone else, his father will begin the beatings again, and both of them will laugh at her."

"She will have died working," said Veretitsyn.

"But if she'd been free, she'd be alive, she'd be happy!"

"How so?"

"Here, like this!" answered Lolenka, waving her hand at her surroundings. "She'd have been working for all people—a large circle!"

"Have you ever noticed how, on water, larger circles are weaker than smaller ones?"

"Oh, no poetic analogies!"

"But is this really"—he also waved his hand at her surroundings—"is this really working for all people?"

"Of course it isn't labor on a world scale," rejoined Lolenka, "but I dare to think that it's also a part of that labor; at least, I'm making my contribution; I serve the mind. . . ."

"Sofya teaches her children—"

"You're poeticizing because you're still in love with her," interrupted Lolenka, starting to laugh. "'Her fair-haired head, their curly little heads. . . .'¹ But looking at it from a present-day point of view, what is it? Slavery, the family! . . . A more elevated woman is subjugated to some nice fellow; she sacrificed herself at the whim of her egotistical mother; she reconciled—that is, reunited again— two bad people so they could cause even more harm together! Somehow, amid the constraints, despite the derision, she passes something humane on to the children. . . . But is it really humane, is it healthy? She passes on to them the same unfortunate precepts of selflessness that are destroying her! Precepts of submission to tyranny! . . . She's guilty, your Sofya! She serves evil, teaches evil. She's training victims! She should understand this."

"She understands that the best mother knows how to educate martyrs."

"Is this really you? I ask in my turn," exclaimed Lolenka. "You've forgotten, but I remember; you were the first to speak the first word of freedom to me—is that you now?"

"I remember exactly," answered Veretitsyn. "I spoke to you, but it was a word of freedom, not separation. . . ."

"Separation?"

"Yes You're alone. Do you understand that?"

"I know I'm alone. A rational being must know how to be alone."

"When you have to be alone," rejoined Veretitsyn. "But when there are still people—"

"They don't exist for me," she interrupted, becoming incensed. "You didn't know it then, but you could have guessed what my life was like, what kind of people I had around me. You made me understand them for the first time. I trusted you. . . . Don't you know that I loved you? Yes, as I never loved again! I understood what kind of yoke love is, how it makes you look at things through someone else's eyes, disappear before someone else's will. I'll never fall in love again; I don't have time—it's foolish. Then, at least, it was still propitious: the strength to free myself arose in me. Injustice, my persecution, had reached an extreme. They had even proposed a husband for me! . . . I decided to run away. Now I would escape to the streets—then I was still searching for a refuge. I wrote my aunt; I didn't even have the money for postage! I'll never forget the humiliation of begging for it in tears from the maid, bowing almost to the ground. . . . Didn't I have the right to wish to escape, to come to hate the memory of the past?"

"No one has a right to judge your running away. You had the right to escape, but never to hate. If you understood more than those people, you should be able to forgive—"

"You never said that!" interrupted Lolenka. "You advocated complete separation! This is a rebirth, too! Is this you? I will ask a thousand times. . . ."

"It's I," repeated Veretitsyn, "but since then a great deal of time has passed."

"And the years have subdued you? . . . Old age?"

"Yes, people become quieter over the years."

"More patient?"

"Smarter."

"Oh! If only someone, someone, would repeat to you now what you said then!" exclaimed Lolenka.

"The extremes?" he asked. "Perhaps. But when you give up several years to reflection you can evaluate whether extremes are useful. You abandon them involuntarily. . . ."

"And become reconciled?"

"You forgive."

"That is, a step backward to the old ways again?" cried Lolenka.

"Why? Forgiving, no longer reproaching, no longer remembering—"

"Yes, perhaps this is very lofty," she interrupted coldly, "but the insulted one, the one who understood that only he himself, his courage, was responsible for preventing him from being destroyed, doesn't forget so easily, doesn't forgive so easily. . . . But this is a matter of personalities: enough about me. I vowed I'd never give anyone power over me again. I won't serve this barbaric old law by example or word. . . . On the contrary, I say to everyone: Do as I have done, free yourselves, all who have hands and a strong will! Live alone—here's life—work, knowledge, and freedom. . . ."

"And what's left for the heart?" Veretitsyn asked softly.

"Are you happy with yours?" she asked derisively.

"But you're also unfortunate," he rejoined. "Ours might ache, but it exists; you don't even have one."

"Ours?" repeated Lolenka. "Yours and Sophie's?"

"You don't understand her," Veretitsyn said gently. "Don't laugh. You summon everyone to freedom, and according to your convictions, which indeed didn't come easily, from your point of view, in large part also correct, you are right. But you are far from Sofya's perfection! Without suffering, you easily earn for yourself a peaceful way of life, entertainment, the affability of your little circle. Meanwhile you serve society with very pleasant work. But your work is still only half work, and even less. . . . Sofya took everything upon herself. She set out to teach goodness and truth with no assurance of success, with only a belief in her work. She set out against vulgarity, egotism, the half educated, insults, cruelty; she set out the way martyrs have gone to profess their faith and meet their death! This is the final fulfillment of responsibility which imposes a consciousness of truth and thirst for goodness! There's no higher deed in our age. It's not even a model: only a woman who desires the highest perfection can attempt it, who feels the strength within herself to serve truth, her own beliefs, to serve fully, willingly, joyfully, forgetting herself. . . . Do the Sisters of Mercy[12] amaze you? Do you cry out in rapture at those women who hand cartridges to their husbands and loved ones in time of war? This isn't any easier; the courage needed is no less; it's no less scandalous; there's no fervor here, no approval from all around; the cause isn't magnificent in appearance and lasts a long time—for life."

"You love her very much," said Lolenka.

Veretitsyn didn't answer and stood up. The clock struck seven.

"You see," he said finally, "here it is, the much extolled free life, because now, at the present, it's the same for you and me. The time has come, going our separate ways, without finishing our conversation; there's never any time for feeling, never time for remembering. We're free people, slaves of the work we've taken upon our shoulders . . . many may love it, but the majority merely persuade themselves that they do, and only a few selected individuals (including myself) speak frankly, that any cause is like a dose of opium and a means to keep on living always for the cause. . . . There are no joys for us. There can be no love: there's no time. . . . Instead, we take up anything that comes along, which lacks any goal or meaning. . . . This is what's called getting older."

"Not true!" Lolenka replied. "Work and knowledge don't grow old because they're eternal."

"Maybe, if you don't notice that part of the soul—feeling—is already dead or lying incapacitated by a stroke. It's possible to deceive oneself."

"I don't want to deceive myself. So what! Then so be it."

"I wish you happiness!"

"And are you happy? . . ."

"It's time for me to go, Elena Vasilyevna."

She hurriedly glanced at the clock.

"Well, good-bye. Come on Tuesday; I'll introduce you to my aunt and also some nice people. Will you come?"

"I don't have time. . . . If I can manage it."

Lolenka accompanied him to the staircase with a candle and returned to her room; and without hesitating even for a moment, she moved an armchair up to the desk and got out a notebook and dictionary, and soon only the ticking of the clock, the sound of a smoldering coal falling in the fireplace, and the scratching of a pen on paper could be heard in the room. . . .

Introduction

The epigraph is from V. Porechnikov (another of Nadezhda Khvoshchin-skaya's pseudonyms), "Provintsial'nye pis'ma o nashei literature: [Pis'mo] VI: Rasskazy zhenshchin o zhenshchinakh," *Otechestvennye zapiski* 145, no. 11 (1862): 51. (This and all subsequent translations are my own.)

1. A number of recent studies in English have begun to examine the historical context for women's writing in Russia. For a broad historical introduction to women writers in Russia, see Barbara Heldt, *Terrible Perfection* (Bloomington: Indiana University Press, 1987); Marina Ledkovsky, Charlotte Rosenthal, and Mary F. Zirin, eds., *A Dictionary of Russian Women Writers* (Westport, Conn.: Greenwood Press, 1994); Catriona Kelly, *A History of Russian Women's Writing, 1820–1992* (Oxford: Clarendon, 1994).

2. Pavlova is the only woman writer who published her work before the twentieth century to receive consistent, continued recognition in anthologies and literary histories until the present time.

3. Sofya Khvoshchinskaya (1828–65) adopted the pseudonym Ivan Vesenev to publish her fictional work; Praskovya Khvoshchinskaya (1832–1916) wrote under the pseudonym S. Zimarova. Another sister died at age eleven.

4. The reality of hostility and condescension toward women writers in Russian society must have strongly influenced Khvoshchinskaya's decision to adopt masculine pseudonyms. Praskovya Khvoshchinskaya explains her sister's use of pseudonyms in her introduction to the 1892 edition of her sister's collected works, noting that "not only in the provinces where every step, every word is judged, but even in the capital women writers were

considered indecorous and unladylike and hid behind pseudonyms." See Nadezhda Khvoshchinskaya, *Sobranie sochinenii* (St. Petersburg: Izd. A. S. Suvorina, 1892), 1:ii. For a look at the use of pseudonyms among world authors that includes many Russian women writers as well, see V. G. Dmitriev, *Skryvshie svoe imya: Iz istorii psevdonimov i anonimov* (Moscow: Nauka, 1970).

5. For more about Khvoshchinskaya's literary and artistic friends and acquaintances, see V. Semevsky, "N. D. Khvoshchinskaya-Zaionchkovskaya (V. Krestovsky-psevdonim)," *Russkaya mysl'* no. 10 (1890): 76–77; no. 12 (1890): 144.

6. Semevsky, "Khvoshchinskaya-Zaionchkovskaya," no. 10: 67.

7. Semevsky, "Khvoshchinskaya-Zaionchkovskaya," no. 10: 67–68.

8. Petr Boborykin (1836–1921) attested to the popularity of Khvoshchinskaya's works with readers in an article for *Novosti* in 1889. He was acquainted with Khvoshchinskaya for over twenty years, beginning in the late 1860s. Noting the popularity of her work during his youth, he commented: "When we were still finishing up our coursework at the gymnasium, Khvoshchinskaya's novels were eagerly read in the provinces, more so by women than by men." See Semevsky, "Khvoshchinskaya-Zaionchkovskaya," no. 10: 61.

9. In his 1856 review of Khvoshchinskaya's novel *The Last Act of the Comedy* (*Poslednee deistvie komedii*), Nikolay Nekrasov commented that "if there was less 'literariness' and more life in Krestovsky's novels, they would arguably be the best works of our most recent literature." Summarizing his strongest objections to her work, he noted: "Philosophy and wit transformed into intellectualizing—here's the basic defect; what's more, thanks to this, with all their merits, Krestovsky's novels are boring." See N. A. Nekrasov, "Zametki o zhurnalakh za mart 1856," in *Polnoe sobranie sochinenii i pisem* (Moscow: Gos. izd-vo khudozhestvennoi literatury, 1950), 9:396–97. See also A. M. Skabichevsky, "Volny russkogo progressa," *Otechestvennye zapiski*, no. 1, pt. 2 (1872)· 7. Skabichevsky alludes to the narrow domestic focus of Khvoshchinskaya's fiction, criticizing her work for "narrowness in its field of observation on one hand and, what's worse, narrowness in the author's own worldview on the other." For more recent

critical responses to Khvoshchinskaya's work and career, see Arja Rosenholm, "Auf den Spuren des Vergessens: Zur Rezeptionsgeschichte der russischen Schriftstellerin N. D. Chvoščinskaja," *Studia Slavica Finlandensia* 6 (1989): 63–91; Karla Thomas Solomon, "Nadezhda Khvoshchinskaia, (1824–1889)," in *Russian Women Writers*, ed. Christine D. Tomei (New York: Garland Publishing, 1999), 261–83; Jehanne Gheith, *(Not) Writing Like a Russian Girl: Evgeniia Tur, V. Krestovskii, and Nineteenth-Century Women's Prose* (Evanston: Northwestern University Press, forthcoming).

10. E. Tur, "Po povodu romana V. Krestovskogo—*V ozhidanii luchshego,*" *Russkaya rech'* no. 12 (1861): 181.

11. M. E. Saltykov, "'Moya sud'ba' M. Kamskoi," in *M. E. Saltykov-Shchedrin: O literature i iskusstve: Izbrannye stat'i, retsenzii, pis'ma* (Moscow: Iskusstvo, 1953), 133. Khvoshchinskaya first met Saltykov when he was vice governor in Ryazan from 1858 to 1860. The two later developed a close, lifelong friendship.

12. A. Reitblat notes that Khvoshchinskaya received the third highest honorarium (paid in rubles per signature) for work published in the 1870s, ranked just behind Tolstoy and Turgenev. She received the twelfth highest maximum honorarium in the 1860s. Reitblat also lists Khvoshchinskaya's name among those contemporary authors whose work was most frequently selected for instructional purposes in schools from the mid-1850s. Her fiction was among the most highly read according to surveys of Moscow libraries in 1860. See A. Reitblat, *Ot Bovy k Bal'montu* (Moscow: Izd-vo MPI, 1991), 70, 88.

13. M. Protopopov, "Geroi nashego vremeni," *Russkoe bogatstvo* no. 3 (1880): 1–2.

14. Semevsky, "Khvoshchinskaya-Zaionchkovskaya," no. 12: 138.

15. M. Tsebrikova, "Ocherk zhizni N. D. Khvoshchinskoi-Zaionchkovskoi (V. Krestovskogo psevdonima)," *Mir Bozhii*, no. 12, pt. 1 (1897): 36.

16. Sundays were established as class holidays at the Smolnyi Institute in 1852. Even before 1864 the students had the privilege, with the permission of the headmistress, of leaving the school's grounds for holidays and Sundays to go home or visit relatives. For more on life at the institutes, see

N. P. Cherepnin, *Imperatorskoe vospitatel'noe obshchestvo blagorodnykh devits: Istoricheskii ocherk, 1764–1914*, 3 vols. (Petrograd: Gos. tip., 1914–15).

There is some evidence that institute life was less restrictive than it has often been portrayed and that many of the girls remembered the institutes very positively. See the selections on Levshina and Rzhevskaya in Robin Bisha et al., eds., *Russian Women: Experience and Expression: An Anthology of Sources* (Bloomington: Indiana University Press, forthcoming). Sofya Khvoshchinskaya published an account of her institute education in 1864. For an English translation of excerpts, see Sofya Khvoshchinskaya, "Reminiscences of Institute Life," in *Russia through Women's Eyes: Autobiographies from Tsarist Russia*, ed. Toby W. Clyman and Judith Vowles (New Haven, Conn.: Yale University Press, 1996), 75–108.

17. For more detailed studies about the historical development of women's education in Russia during the eighteenth and nineteenth centuries, see J. L. Black, "Educating Women in Eighteenth-Century Russia," in *Citizens for the Fatherland* (Boulder, Colo.: East European Quarterly, 1979), 152–72; Sophie Satina, *The Education of Women in Pre-Revolutionary Russia*, trans. A. F. Poustchine (New York: n.p., 1966); Elena Osipovna Likhacheva, *Materialy dlya istorii zhenskogo obrazovaniya v Rossii*, 3 vols. (St. Petersburg: Tip. Stesyulevicha, 1899–1901); Christine Johanson, *Women's Struggle for Higher Education in Russia, 1855–1900* (Kingston: McGill-Queen's University Press, 1987).

18. Many radical groups became more subversive after 1848, considering revolution as the only means for introducing change in Russia. One of these groups, the Petrashevtsy, initially a literary circle, included writers Mikhail Saltykov and Fedor Dostoevsky. The government arrested ten members of this group (including Dostoevsky) on December 22, 1849, exiling them to the Caucasus and Siberia. For more on the Petrashevtsy and the Russian revolutionary movement at this time, see J. H. Seddon, *The Petrashevtsy: A Study of the Russian Revolutionaries of 1848* (Manchester: Manchester University Press, 1985).

19. A surgeon and educator, Nikolay Pirogov organized the Sisters of Mercy of the Society of the Exaltation of the Cross, who served as nurses during the Crimean War. Pirogov later published an article entitled

"Questions of Life." His essay, which criticized the superficiality of women's education, brought the "woman question" to the forefront of public attention. For a closer look at the evolution of the issues associated with the "woman question" in Russia, see Richard Stites, *The Women's Liberation Movement in Russia, 1860–1930* (Princeton, N.J.: Princeton University Press, 1978); Victor Ripp, *Turgenev's Russia* (Ithaca: Cornell University Press, 1980); Barbara Alpern Engel, *Mothers and Daughters: Women of the Intelligentsia in Nineteenth-Century Russia* (Cambridge: Cambridge University Press, 1983).

20. V. Porechnikov [Nadezhda Khvoshchinskaya], "Provintsial'nye pis'ma o nashei literature: Pis'mo tret'e," *Otechestvennye zapiski* 142, no. 5 (1862): 43.

21. The high incidence of book and library crimes among nineteenth-century Russian literary heroines suggests various analogous antecedents linking the acquisition of knowledge with crime, such as the theft of forbidden fruit in the biblical Garden of Eden, the myth of Prometheus, and the Faust legend. Pushkin especially emphasizes the illicit nature of Tatyana's reading habits in *Eugene Onegin*. In chapter 2 the reader learns that Tatyana sometimes hides a "secret" (*tainyi*) volume under her pillow. Later, in chapter 3, the reader observes her again wandering alone with a "dangerous" (*opasnoi*) book. Odoevsky reports instances of library crime in his "Princess Zizi" ("Knyazhna Zizi") (1839). His heroine writes to her friend Masha unabashedly about "stealing" (*krast'*) books from her father's library. Netochka, the heroine of Dostoevsky's unfinished novel *Netochka Nezvanova* (1849), discovers the key to her benefactors' library, helping herself in secret to books over a period of several years. Book and library crimes appear in the work of many women writers as well. Elena Gan's heroine Anyuta in "A Futile Gift" ("Naprasnyi dar") (1842) disobeys her male mentor Geilfreind, perusing forbidden volumes of poetry without his knowledge. Khvoshchinskaya's Lolenka in *The Boarding-School Girl* receives a copy of *Romeo and Juliet* from her male mentor, Veretitsyn, which she then carefully conceals from her parents.

22. My own brief summary of the novel is necessarily simplistic. For more on Tatyana's reading practices and the relationship between life and

literature in *Eugene Onegin,* see William Mills Todd III, *"Eugene Onegin:* 'Life's Novel,'" in *Literature and Society in Imperial Russia, 1800–1914,* ed. William Mills Todd III (Stanford: Stanford University Press, 1978), 203–35. Todd argues convincingly that Tatyana achieves skill in interpreting cultural convention in her reading throughout the course of the novel, permitting greater mastery over her environment. Todd gives considerable weight to Eugene's unknowing role as Tatyana's mentor. As she peruses the books in his library in his absence, she is guided in her reading by Eugene's annotations and fingernail marks on the text. See also Richard Gregg, "Rhetoric in Tat'jana's Last Speech: The Camouflage That Reveals," *SEEJ* 25, no. 1 (1981): 1–12. Gregg, too, emphasizes Tatyana's mastery of literary convention as reflected through her use of different rhetorical styles in the novel's last chapter. See also Joe Andrew, "Mothers and Daughters in Russian Literature of the First Half of the Nineteenth Century," *SEER* 73, no. 1 (1995): 37–60. Andrew examines the scant references in *Eugene Onegin* to Tatyana's mother for evidence of her influence on her daughter's life decisions as well as her choice of reading.

23. A. S. Pushkin, *Eugene Onegin: A Novel in Verse,* trans. James E. Falen (Carbondale: Southern Illinois University Press, 1990), 4.26.104.

24. Khvoshchinskaya's analysis of the male mentor figure in the previously quoted third letter of her "Provincial Letters about Our Literature" specifically mentions Pushkin's novel in verse (41–42). Khvoshchinskaya probably had *Eugene Onegin* in mind when she wrote *The Boarding-School Girl.* Lolenka displays traits characteristic of both Tatyana and Olga; her taste for forbidden books recalls Tatyana's illicit reading pleasures, while her name recalls the diminutive form of the name Olga—Olenka. Khvoshchinskaya briefly mentions Tatyana in this essay to contrast attitudes and behavior of girls past and present.

25. Ivan Goncharov, *Oblomov,* trans. Ann Dunnigan (New York: New American Library, 1963), 512.

26. Although I discuss only a few examples of the male mentor figure in any detail here, others may be found in Dostoevsky's *Poor Folk* (1846), Alexander Herzen's *Who Is to Blame?* (1847), and Nikolay Chernyshevsky's *What Is to Be Done?* (1864). A number of women writers also treated this

subject. Khvoshchinskaya considers the depiction of the male mentor in Zhadovskaya's (1824–83) "Otstalaya" ("The Backward Girl") (1861) in one of her critical essays. See Porechnikov, "Provintsial'nye pis'ma," 24–52. For more about the male mentor figure in Russian nineteenth-century literature, see also Irina Paperno, *Chernyshevsky and the Age of Realism* (Stanford: Stanford University Press, 1988), and Catriona Kelly, *A History of Russian Women's Writing, 1820–1992* (Oxford: Clarendon Press, 1994), 65–66.

27. Veretitsyn quotes the original German title of Lanner's waltz "Hoffnungs Strahlen" ("Rays of Hope") incorrectly, omitting the genitive case ending to the word "Hoffnung." While possibly a misprint, reproduced in every edition of the novella, other evidence suggests that the error was self-consciously included in the text. While the expression "rays of hope" also occurs in Russian as *luchi nadezhdy*, Lolenka immediately responds that the name seems "strange" as soon as she hears it. While the title may perhaps seem unusual to her for a waltz, Veretitsyn's strange pronunciation would more likely elicit her sudden exclamation of surprise.

28. Veretitsyn overhears Lolenka reading "The Voice of a Patriot on the Taking of Warsaw" ("Glas patriota na vzyatie Varshava"), a poem written in 1794 by the Russian poet Ivan Ivanovich Dmitriev (1760–1837), in her garden early in the novella but later apparently mistakes the author for Kheraskov. When he recalls that Lolenka enjoyed reading Kheraskov, she responds: "Not at all!" Since apparently each of Lolenka's visits to the garden is indicated in the novella, her response to his comment suggests that either he has mistaken Kheraskov for Dmitriev, she did not enjoy her reading, or she does not remember that she enjoyed her reading. The latter two hypotheses seem less likely since the reader also knows that Lolenka used to enjoy her studies and that she has a good memory. Other suggestions of Veretitsyn's poor knowledge retention occur throughout the text. In chapter 11 Veretitsyn tells Sofya, "If it wasn't for your books, I'd have forgotten how to read." He apparently has forgotten that Ibrayev sent him a large number of books at the beginning of the second chapter of the novella.

29. For an overview of the responses of Russian women writers to various aspects of the "woman question" that includes an examination of *The*

Boarding-School Girl or other works by Khvoshchinskaya, see Jane Cost-
low, "Love, Work and the Woman Question in Mid Nineteenth-Century
Women's Writing," in *Women Writers in Russian Literature*, ed. Toby W.
Clyman and Diana Greene (Westport, Conn.: Praeger, 1994), 61–75; Arja
Rosenholm, "The 'Woman Question' of the 1860s and the Ambiguity of
the 'Learned Woman,'" in *Gender and Russian Literature: New Perspectives*,
ed. and trans. Rosalind Marsh (Cambridge: Cambridge University Press,
1996), 112–28.

30. Mary Zirin also notes Khvoshchinskaya's use of needlework as a re-
current motif in novels like *In Hope of Something Better* (*V ozhidanii
luchshego*) (1860) in her essay "Women's Prose Fiction in the Age of Realism," in *Women Writers in Russian Literature*, ed. Toby W. Clyman and
Diana Greene (Westport, Conn.: Praeger, 1994), 77–94. There are numerous examples of this motif throughout Khvoshchinskaya's prose. Natalya
Alekseevna in *The Healthy Ones* (*Zdorovye*) (1883) tells her male guest that
she's sewing something for her daughter, something she might just keep
for herself, but something she never identifies to the reader or to her guest.
The female protagonist of the novel *Vstrecha* (*An Encounter*) (1860), continually occupied with her needlework, misunderstands the intent of her
male guest's request that she put her work aside to talk: "Don't you like the
design? Wait and see how it turns out when it's finished."

31. Khvoshchinskaya's use of this stylistic feature, also termed "free indirect discourse" or "narrated monologue," recalls the work of Flaubert,
Dostoevsky, and Jane Austen. For more on the use of free indirect discourse in the nineteenth-century novel, see Roy Pascal, *The Dual Voice:
Free Indirect Speech and Its Functioning in the Nineteenth-Century European
Novel* (Manchester: Manchester University Press, 1977). A number of re-
cent studies focus specifically on the function of narrative voice in the work
of women writers, including the use of free indirect discourse. See, for ex-
ample, Carol J. Singley and Susan Elizabeth Sweeney, eds., *Anxious
Power: Reading, Writing, and Ambivalence in Narrative by Women* (Albany:
State University of New York Press, 1993), and Susan Lanser, *Fictions of
Authority: Women Writers and Narrative Voice* (Ithaca: Cornell University
Press, 1992). The landmark text by Sandra Gilbert and Susan Gubar, *The*

Madwoman in the Attic (New Haven, Conn.: Yale University Press, 1979), identifies numerous similarities among nineteenth-century women writers in narrative technique, choice of images and themes, and the use of pseudonyms—all relevant for examining Khvoshchinskaya's work.

32. Semevsky, "Khvoshchinskaya-Zaionchkovskaya," no. 10: 85–86.

Chapter I

1. Khvoshchinskaya follows the example of earlier Russian writers, situating her novella in an imaginary city designated only by a single letter.

2. Aleksander Peresvet was one of two monks sent by Abbot Sergius of Radonezh to accompany forces battling Tatar domination west of the Volga River. He was killed around midday on September 8, 1380, in one-to-one combat with the Tatar warrior Temir-murza. It was believed that such combat would foretell the outcome of a later battle. According to legend, Peresvet's death preceded the battle of Kulikovo, which occurred later that day and proved a major victory for Russian forces over Tatar domination in the region.

3. The Nobles' Assembly was a provincial legislative body, but the name also referred to a kind of club. The Nobles' Assembly arranges a ball in "Princess Mary" in Lermontov's *Hero of Our Time*.

4. Veretitsyn is probably referring to the wife of the provincial governor. Apparently a princess as well, she may imagine her position to be equivalent in importance to the czar's wife.

5. A hollow-bodied three-stringed wooden folk instrument used by minstrels in Russia during Kievan times, the *gudok* was oval or pear shaped and had a short neck and flat soundboard. Still found in southern Russia and the Ukraine in the eighteenth century, the instrument had largely disappeared by the nineteenth century. The term *gudok* also refers to a common kind of reed pipe.

6. *Le jeune malheureux* translates as "the unfortunate young man."

7. A pelerine is a cape, usually with ends coming to points in the front. Tulle is a fine netting used in veils or dresses, commonly made of silk.

8. The Russian word *Liudovik* can mean either "Louis" or "Ludwig." Subsequent references in the novella to the marquise de Pompadour and the "Louises" reveal that Lolenka is studying French history.

9. Lolenka's school is named for a woman, apparently a private citizen. Graduates of the government-operated institutes often established private boarding schools. The fact that the school's name is readily recognized by Veretitsyn may indicate the prestige of this particular school. Lolenka is probably a day student, since later references in the text reveal that the school is within walking distance of her home.

10. I did not find a source for this. In addition, this line has been altered in some later editions of *The Boarding-School Girl*. The phrase that appeared in the text that was first published in 1861 in *Notes of the Fatherland* and then reprinted in 1892 in Khvoshchinskaya's *Collected Works* as *ne sovershiv lovitvy* was substituted in some editions by the phrase *ne sovershiv molitvy*—"without having finished their prayers." The word *lovitva* is no longer in current usage, although it appears in the work of other nineteenth-century authors such as Pushkin.

Chapter II

1. A droshky is a low, usually uncovered summer carriage.

2. Sofya probably visits the garrets—attic rooms or apartments that provide cheap housing for the poor—only through charity work.

Chapter III

1. *Lucia di Lammermoor,* an opera in three acts by Gaetano Donizetti, premiered in Naples September 26, 1835. The story was based on a novel by Sir Walter Scott (1771–1832), *The Bride of Lammermoor,* first published in 1819. A reference to this opera also appears in Gustave Flaubert's *Madame Bovary* (1856). Listening to the music, Emma recalls reading Scott in her youth.

2. Josef Franz Lanner (1801–43) was an Austrian composer.

3. The title of Lanner's waltz is misspelled in every edition of *The Boarding-School Girl* that I consulted, including the text originally published in *Notes of the Fatherland*. The correct spelling is "Hoffnungs Strahlen" ("Rays of Hope").

4. The institutes originally accommodated four grade levels of three years each. If Lolenka's boarding school follows this model, Lolenka is probably in the first class or year at the highest grade level in her boarding

school. The first-year class would likely include students aged fourteen to fifteen; the second-year class would include students aged fifteen to sixteen; the third-year class would include students aged sixteen to seventeen. Later in the novella Lolenka's mother expresses her hope that her daughter will be able to skip ahead early to the final class. In that case, she must complete only one more year before graduating from school.

Chapter IV

1. Nikolay Koshansky (1781–1831) was the author of two rhetoric texts, *The General Rhetoric* and *The Specialized Rhetoric,* used in Russian schools for most of the nineteenth century. Lolenka is probably studying *The General Rhetoric* in class, since she is memorizing the definitions of stylistic devices such as metaphor, synecdoche, and metonymy. *The Specialized Rhetoric* analyzes specific types of writing such as letters, dialogue, narration, and oratory. Both works contained numerous examples from literature and history.

2. Lolenka is reciting an excerpt from the 1794 poem "The Voice of a Patriot on the Taking of Warsaw" by Ivan Ivanovich Dmitriev.

3. If Lolenka is reading an excerpt from Dmitriev's "The Voice of a Patriot on the Taking of Warsaw," the next and therefore last line of that stanza would be "A Bashkir with well-aimed arrows." The last line of the poem is "Where the whole world is the limit!"

4. I did not find a source for this.

5. Veretitsyn may be alluding to a maxim or proverb similar to this old English proverb, which outlines the features of exemplary feminine behavior: "Maidens must be mild and meek, swift to hear and slow to speak."

Chapter V

1. The game of knucklebones is played with cured knucklebones or stones. In one version, bones are placed side by side in a row. The player throws a master bone, filled with lead for extra weight, at the remaining bones. The children are fighting for possession of these prized, lead-filled bones.

2. Kvass is a fermented drink usually made from rye or barley malt and rye flour, sometimes also with fruits and berries.

3. Lolenka's mother addresses her by one of her nicknames, Alyona. Lolenka is also referred to by other nicknames throughout the novella, such as Lolya, as well as the French form of her name, Hélène, and the Russian formal equivalent, Elena.

Chapter VI

1. The exam is oral, and each student awaits her turn to answer a question.

2. Veretitsyn sees Ibrayev's name transliterated from the Russian Cyrillic as "Ybrayev."

Chapter VII

1. The talented and beautiful Marquise de Pompadour (Jeanna Antoinette Poisson, 1721–64) was a mistress of French king Louis XV from 1745 to 1750. Lolenka apparently is quoting from her textbook.

2. A *pirog* is a meat or vegetable pie; it can also be a fruit-filled pie or pastry.

Chapter VIII

1. *Peau de soie* was a term used in the second half of the nineteenth century to refer to a somewhat thick silk with a dull satiny texture on both sides. A mantilla is a large veil worn over the head and shoulders or a small cape.

2. Veretitsyn calls her familiarly by a nickname, Lolenka, instead of a more formal form of address.

3. "Cacography" refers to poor handwriting or incorrect spelling. The students are given selections with intentionally placed errors, which they are then asked to correct. The question concerns a part of speech—the past participle.

4. The Orthodox ecclesiastical day begins at sunset the previous day. Eight "hours" or services are distributed evenly throughout the day and night. In monasteries, matins usually occurs from 3:00 to 6:00 A.M., followed by the service for "first hour" from 6:00 to 9:00 A.M. Early-morning lay services usually combine matins and "first hour" from 6:00 to 9:00 A.M. The text probably refers to the beginning of the morning service itself at 6:00 A.M.

Chapter IX

1. The position of deacon occupied a clerical ranking just beneath that of priest. Sexton was also a low-ranking position, though outside the hierarchy that included deacons, priests, and bishops. After 1868 sextons were no longer considered part of the clergy at all.

2. Veretitsyn probably is referring to the February coup of 1848 that deposed King Louis Philippe of France. Louis Napoleon Bonaparte was elected president of the Second Republic that following December. After extending the presidential term from four to ten years, he established the Second Empire in 1852 and took the title Napoleon III. He ruled as absolute monarch until ousted by the Republicans in 1870 during the Franco-Prussian War.

Chapter X

1. The clerk's name day would be the feast day associated with the saint for whom he is named.

2. This fortepiano is a smaller instrument probably designed for instructional purposes. The sourdine is used to muffle the sound.

3. François René de Chateaubriand (1768–1848) was a French Romantic writer.

4. Although Lolenka is reading *Romeo and Juliet* in French, all quotations from Shakespeare in *The Boarding-School Girl* are in Russian, as if Lolenka is translating the remembered French lines into Russian in her mind. The original line from act 2, scene 2, of *Romeo and Juliet* reads: "What's in a name? that which we call a rose / By any other name would smell as sweet."

5. The original line from act 2, scene 2, of *Romeo and Juliet* reads: "Romeo doff thy name; / And for that name, which is no part of thee, / Take all myself."

6. The original line from *Romeo and Juliet* at the end of act 1, scene 5, is: "My only love sprung from my only hate!"

7. There is no single line in *Romeo and Juliet* that corresponds exactly to the line recited by Lolenka. The closest match is a phrase spoken by

Romeo at the end of act 1, scene 4, as he prepares to leave for the Capulets' banquet: "I fear too early; for my mind misgives / Some consequence, yet hanging in the stars."

Chapter XI

1. Originally unbleached, blond lace now is bleached white or dyed black. A background of fine threaded mesh is woven together with floral patterns made of a soft, heavy thread. Also called silk bobbin lace.

2. Petersburg is crisscrossed by river channels and canals that form numerous islands. Vasilevsky Island is one of forty or so such islands in Petersburg and is part of the Baltic shoreline. There are a series of streets called "lines" that crisscross the main streets or prospects.

3. A covering or lining, *double* here refers to a fashionable coat covering.

4. Dried linden blossoms are used medicinally to help reduce fever. They are also used in a gargle.

5. Military forces commanded by Napoleon III contributed to a victory over Russia in the Crimean War (1853–56). Seeking to expand its territory, Russia competed with the Ottoman empire for territory in the Balkans but also challenged British concerns in the region. France entered the war in support of Roman Catholic interest in the holy places of Turkish controlled Palestine. Both Britain and France declared war on Russia in 1854.

6. Prison hulks were ships built to serve as floating prisons. Retired ship skeletons were also used for the same purpose.

7. Veretitsyn may be referring to a much quoted line in the New Testament, Romans 1:9: "Without ceasing I make mention of you always in my prayers."

8. A card game for three, preference became popular in Eastern Europe during the eighteenth century. Although the responsibility for dealing the cards is restricted to three players, the game is often played with four, each player dealing in turn but sitting out his own deal.

Chapter XII

1. The original line from act 2, scene 2, of *Romeo and Juliet* reads: "Love goes toward love, as schoolboys from their books."

2. The Fast of St. Peter lasts from Trinity Monday (the day after All Saints' Day) until June 29. All Saints' Day is the Sunday after Whitsuntide in the Eastern Church. Whitsuntide lasts for a week beginning on the seventh Sunday, or fiftieth day, after Easter. Controversy generated over the date of Easter was finally resolved only in A.D. 325 by the decree of the Council of Nicaea. The date is computed to coincide with the first Sunday after the vernal equinox.

3. Pelageya may be referring to icons or frescoes on the church walls, or illustrations in church books depicting the lives and martyrdom of the saints, scenes of sin, damnation, and redemption.

4. The *Tale of Prince Bova* was a popular chivalric romance in Russia from the seventeenth century up until the beginning of the twentieth century that originated in France during the time of the Crusades. In the story, the hero, Prince Bova, battles to obtain his inheritance from an evil stepmother who has killed his father. Succeeding in the end, he marries Princess Druzhevna.

5. The Assumption of the Virgin Mary (her ascent into heaven at the end of her life) is celebrated on August 15.

6. A coarse silk fabric made from a good grade of silk waste, *bourre de soie* is a by-product of the silk-manufacturing process.

Chapter XIII

1. The Hermitage is one of the largest museums in the world. It contains a rich treasury of Western European painting, coins, books, jewelry, and archaeological artifacts.

2. Bartolomé Esteban Murillo (1618?-82) was a Spanish artist. The painting viewed by Veretitsyn in the Hermitage is probably *San Juanito y el cordero* (*The Child St. John and the Lamb*) and depicts Saint John as a boy with his arms encircling the neck of a lamb. The painting owned by the Hermitage is a copy. The original is in the National Gallery in London.

3. Veretitsyn is probably looking at the painting *Jesús niño i San Juanito abrazándole* (*The Young Jesus and the Young Saint John Embracing Him*). The Hermitage owns a copy of this work. The original is in Madrid's Royal Palace.

4. Domenichino (Domenico Zampieri, 1581-1641) was an Italian artist and architect. The only painting by Domenichino treating a mythological theme owned by the Hermitage is *Venus Sleeping*, a work disputably attributed to both Domenichino and Andrea Sacchi.

5. Andrea del Sarto (Andrea Domenico d'Agnolo di Francesco, 1486-1531) was an Italian painter. The Hermitage owned two very similar paintings of the Madonna during this period. The painting entitled *The Holy Family with St. Elizabeth and John the Baptist* best fits the narrative description, since the figure of the child appears to be almost standing. Of disputed originality during Khvoshchinskaya's time, this painting is now considered a copy of the original in the Louvre. The other painting, *Madonna and Child with SS. Catherine, Elizabeth, and John the Baptist*, depicts an infant supported entirely in his mother's arms.

6. Veretitsyn may be formulating his own version of a precept found in the Gospel of Matthew (7:12), also sometimes called the Golden Rule: "In everything do unto others as you would have them do unto you."

7. The reference is to the fable entitled "Strekoza i muravei" ("The Dragonfly and the Ant"), first published by Ivan Krylov in 1808. A dragonfly, or gadfly, who has spent a carefree summer singing, becomes worried when winter arrives. Approaching an ant who has worked hard during the summer to store food for the long winter, the dragonfly asks for shelter. The rather uncharitable ant responds, "Were you always singing? Now that's an occupation: Well, then go dance!"

8. Mikhail Kheraskov (1733-1807) was an eighteenth-century Russian poet. Veretitsyn may be confusing Dmitriev's poem "The Voice of a Patriot on the Taking of Warsaw" with Kheraskov's epic *Rossiada*. Kheraskov's poem also depicts images of East and West, Christianity and Islam.

9. Jean Baptiste Greuze (1725-1805) was a French painter.

10. *A giorno* is Italian for "brightly," or "as though illuminated by daylight."

11. I did not find a source for this.

12. The Sisters of Mercy, founded in Dublin in 1831, offered education to poor girls. Later the organization became involved in other social ser-

vices and work in hospitals. In Russia, Nikolay Pirogov became famous for supervising a mission of the Sisters of Mercy during the Crimean War. Although the idea of using women in field hospitals at first provoked public disapproval, the women's courageous service helped to change Russian attitudes toward women's roles.